ANDY BRIGGS
VILL@IN.NET

Power
Surge

OXFORD
UNIVERSITY PRESS

OXFORD
UNIVERSITY PRESS

Great Clarendon Street, Oxford OX2 6DP

Oxford University Press is a department of the University of Oxford.
It furthers the University's objective of excellence in research, scholarship,
and education by publishing worldwide in

Oxford   New York

Auckland   Cape Town   Dar es Salaam   Hong Kong   Karachi
Kuala Lumpur   Madrid   Melbourne   Mexico City   Nairobi
New Delhi   Shanghai   Taipei   Toronto

With offices in

Argentina   Austria   Brazil   Chile   Czech Republic   France   Greece
Guatemala   Hungary   Italy   Japan   Poland   Portugal   Singapore
South Korea   Switzerland   Thailand   Turkey   Ukraine   Vietnam

Oxford is a registered trade mark of Oxford University Press
in the UK and in certain other countries

British Library Cataloguing in Publication Data

Data available

ISBN: 978-0-19-272924-8

1 3 5 7 9 10 8 6 4 2

Printed in Great Britain by Cox and Wyman Ltd, Reading, Berkshire

Paper used in the production of this book is a natural,
recyclable product made from wood grown in sustainable forests.
The manufacturing process conforms to the environmental
regulations of the country of origin.

From one noggin to another.

From: Andy Briggs
To: VILLAIN.NET readers everywhere
Subject: Careful on the web!

As you know, the Internet is a brilliant place to explore, but you need to be careful when using it.

In this awesome book, the villains (and heroes!) download their powers from the different websites. But VILLAIN.NET and HERO.COM don't really exist. :-(I invented them when I was dreaming about how cool shooting fireballs would be. The idea for VILLAIN.NET suddenly came to me when I thought of how the sand tentacle grabs hold of . . . Oh wait! You haven't read it yet so I'd better shut up! :-) Anyway, I began writing and before I knew it, the idea had spiralled into HERO.COM as well. But I had to make up all of the Internet stuff. None of it is really out there on the web.

Here are my tips for safe surfing on the web: keep your identity secret (like all good superheroes do), stick to safe websites, make sure a parent, teacher or guardian knows that you're online, don't bully anyone else — that's seriously not good - and if anyone sends you anything that makes you feel uncomfortable, don't reply, and tell an adult you trust.

I do have my own website, and it's totally safe (even without superpowers!): **www.whichsideareyouon.co.uk**

Be safe out there!

:-)

CONTENTS

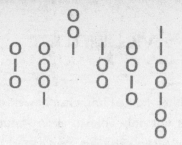

New Kid on the Job

A light drizzle flattened Jake Hunter's spiky blond hair to his scalp. He scowled; no amount of superpowers or wealth could prevent the little things from annoying him, and these days he had trouble keeping his temper. To unleash his anger would be to unleash volatile superpowers that were almost beyond his control.

And they were not a good substitute for a jacket with a hood.

His contact was running late. He glanced around the sprawling expanse of St Mark's Square, which, despite the poor weather, was busy with tourists. The domed Basilica at the end of the piazza made him think of Moscow where his friends had decided to mug him for a case full of money. Then he had been chased by a superhero called Chameleon. That had been fun, although it hadn't felt like it at the time. His nemesis was now a crystalline sculpture in Jake's gothic Transylvanian castle.

Jake mused at how quickly his life had changed since he opened that spam email inviting him to join

Villain.net. Now he had immense powers at his finger-tips. He was not only able to absorb multiple super-powers from Villain.net like a sponge, and amplify their strength, but he could also combine them to create unique powers that had never been seen before.

But the price he paid was an addiction to them.

His DNA had become entangled within the website and now he was cursed to continuously download from Villain.net in order to stay alive.

Both the Hero Foundation and the Council of Evil desperately wanted to probe his powers to use him as a super-weapon. Rather than live a life on the run, Jake had chosen a side and accepted a seat on the Council.

However, he considered it a temporary position.

A man approached him through the crowd. He was huge. It wasn't fat, it was just that his body seemed square. His massive bald head ran straight into his shoulders without the benefit of a neck. He wore expensive high-collared shirts to conceal this fact, but he still attracted stares from gawping tourists. He was a key figure in the Council of Evil and his name was Momentum.

'I hate Venice,' stated the big man as he reached Jake.

Jake shrugged. His list of pet hates was too long to discuss here.

'It gets us away from the Council's prying eyes,' said Jake. 'I don't think they'd approve of what we're 'doing.' They walked towards the cathedral, turning at the large clock tower, and approached the waterfront. 'I wasn't sure you were going to come.'

'Why? Did you think I'd set you up and put you into danger all on your own?'

Jake smiled. 'Why not? I would. I have to admit, I thought you'd back out of our plan.'

Momentum grunted noncommittally. 'I'd be doing this with or without you. We just need to make sure we don't end up like Chromosome.'

Chromosome was the villain Jake had replaced on the Council of Evil. Necros, the unofficial leader of the Council, had discovered her plot to recruit Jake and use his unique powers to overthrow the Council. She had been swiftly eliminated.

'Chromosome was trying to create a team of supporters from within the Council. Of course people were going to betray her. It's stupid to trust so many villains. My plan is a little more . . . subtle.'

Momentum arched an eyebrow—or he would have done if he had possessed any facial hair. 'Really? How subtle?'

'Only you, me, and Mr Grimm know about it. That way, any treachery will be easier to discover.' It was a veiled threat and Jake took some satisfaction when he noticed Momentum shift uncomfortably.

They reached the busy waterway and stopped near

the jetty. It was the Venetian lagoon, which was much wider than the canals in the main part of the city. Other populated islands lay fifty metres offshore, a chain of boats running between them.

Momentum studied Jake. 'And what makes you think I wouldn't betray you?'

'I'm a naturally trusting person,' said Jake with a smile. 'Plus, we're officially in business together. Don't forget, I'm paying you for that other "*thing*".' He held out his hand expectantly.

Momentum hesitated before reaching into his pocket and pulling out an MP3 device. It looked tiny in his hand. Jake took it, examining it closely. He'd paid several million for this small device—money he had been forced to steal from a bank vault. That kind of crime wasn't really his style, but it was an important safety catch in his overall plan.

Not that long ago a powerful ability had been used to wipe not only his family's memories, but also their ability to even see Jake. It had taken the unique powers of a now dead superhero called Psych for him to restore their memories and their ability to see him.

But the victory was short lived.

Mr Grimm had been forced to separate Jake from his family once again before the Enforcers, a non-superpowered combat team, had arrived to arrest him.

New Kid on the Job

Shortly after that, the Council of Evil had offered him a position. The choice was power and glory with them or a stable and average life with his family—but without his powers.

Before Jake could decide, Grimm had delivered more bad news.

His family had been hospitalized. It seems the super-power he had used to restore his parents' memory was not strong enough—he had given them a half dose, it was all he had. They had fallen unconscious, and when they woke, their memories had been lost again—but not completely, as Jake discovered when he went to visit them.

This time, they could see him; they just had *no idea* who he was! Jake was a stranger to them. The police had been called and Jake was, once again, forced to flee from his family home.

Mr Grimm had told him that some of Psych's power had been donated to the Hero Foundation before he died. The Foundation HQ had since been destroyed by Basilisk—the same archfiend who had introduced Jake to Villain.net. However, the last portion of Psych's power now resided inside the most unlikely hero, who was currently in a coma.

With everything stacked against him, Jake accepted the position on the Council of Evil. His old fury had flared up against both the Council of Evil and the Hero

Foundation who had messed up his life. He vowed that once he got his family back, he would destroy both organizations.

This was war.

Jake didn't want to dwell on that, it only made him angry. He pressed 'play'. A stream of white noise poured from the speaker—the high pitched warbling of computer data.

'You're sure this will work?'

'It's a Data-Rendered-Aural-Inhibitor—or a Draizor for short. I stole the technology directly from the Foundation. Pete Kendall is being subliminally conditioned as we speak to reject his heroic leanings. There is a hidden device in his room feeding him instructions at a frequency only he can hear. Those same instructions will also make him susceptible to the Draizor. The data tones on the device in your hand are designed to specifically interfere with the neural-processing of his superpowers.'

Momentum noticed a puzzled expression spread across Jake's face. He dumbed down the explanation. 'The Draizor plays high-pitched tones and a hypnotic voice beyond our ordinary range of hearing that will prevent Pete from using his powers against you. It will cause him pain. Think of it as a safety catch for your lethal weapon.'

Jake slid the Draizor into his jacket. 'And are you going to tell me what your interest is in Pete?'

New Kid on the Job

'Both you and Pete are unique because of the sheer number of powers at your disposal. When Pete smashed through dozens of vats of raw superpowers and absorbed them into his system he became one of the most powerful beings on earth. Unlike you, he can't create new abilities at will, but we think he can manipulate the ones he does possess to a devastating effect.'

Pete's abilities sounded impressive but Jake was only interested in the comatose hero because inside him lay the last surviving sample of Psych's superpowers. Within that power were the memories needed to unlock his parents' amnesia.

Jake sniggered. 'And you think you can use him and his powers like people have tried to use me?' Momentum was free to use Pete however he liked just as soon as Jake got what he wanted.

'I have my plans. We all have our secrets. And I'm not as trusting as you are, Hunter.' The latter comment was laced with sarcasm. 'But I am willing to help you in your crusade against the Council as long as you wish to bring it down and promise not to take the lead position for yourself. I tire of their rules and regulations. Their bureaucracy is making any decent world domination plan a nightmare. Already this year they have turned down twenty-three applications.'

'I want to see the Council fall,' said Jake with determination. They were responsible for turning his life

upside down. Villain.net had hooked him and turned him into a monster.

'Good, because here is our first opportunity.'

Momentum pointed to a large boat that was docking against the jetty. It had a single logo in the corner that Jake instantly recognized as belonging to the Enforcers—the United Nations' private, non-superpowered, army. Since the Hero Foundation's main headquarters had crashed into the Mongolian desert, courtesy of a gang of rogue supervillains, the Foundation had been scrambling to rebuild and update their equipment. The devices they were now using were rapidly leaving the Council of Evil behind in the technology race. Rather than invest millions in researching alternatives, the Council were simply stealing consignments of gadgets as they were being delivered to Foundation facilities, like the one Jake had discovered in Venice.

Once the boat had docked, the rear section was raised on hydraulic rams and four heavily armed Enforcers marched out and took position on the jetty, keeping nosy tourists at bay. To everybody else this looked like a secure bank or gallery transfer that happened regularly across the city. Both the Foundation and Council had discovered that by operating in plain sight nobody asked questions.

The two supervillains knew that on board was a consignment of hi-tech gadgets that were powered by small quantities of superpowers. They had been designed so that nobody had to download many super-powers in one go and they would have more control over them. Momentum thought they were perfect for their plans to defeat the other supers—fellow villains first, followed by the Hero Foundation. Momentum had called it 'a new world order'.

With a bass-heavy rumble, a vehicle glided from the back of the boat and onto the jetty. It was a hovervan—a hybrid between a security van and a hovercraft. Jake hadn't been expecting that.

'Ready?' snarled Momentum, who was already psyching himself up for an attack.

'Go for it,' said Jake, happy to let Momentum do all the hard work.

Momentum charged forward. Each footfall got heav-ier and heavier until the concrete splintered with each impact. The Enforcers immediately spotted the threat and opened fire. Bullets bounced from Momentum's skin, although his thousand-pound suit suffered multi-ple rips and tears.

He clobbered into two of the Enforcers, scattering them like bowling pins. One was hurled into the water, the other spun high into the air, before thumping down onto the jetty.

The hovervan's driver spun round to try and avoid an impact. True to his name, Momentum became almost unstoppable as he built up speed—but as a result his dexterity suffered too. The hovervan had managed to avoid a direct hit, but Momentum still clipped the bumper. Metal crunched under impact and the vehicle spun uncontrollably on its cushion of air—forcing the two Enforcers inside to almost pass out from the sudden G-force.

Momentum skidded to a halt, concrete rucking under his feet as though it was carpet. Tourists were now screaming and running as two Enforcers shot at him. Momentum covered his face and charged again.

Jake watched as the big man dispatched the shooters, but came under fire from others standing on the back of the boat. Momentum was losing his temper and ignored the hovervan—choosing instead to run towards the boat. The carbon-fibre hull shattered as the big man struck. Jake heard the Council member bellow victoriously before the boat shattered like an egg and collapsed into the lagoon taking the villain and the Enforcers under.

As the boat broke apart, the hovervan accelerated into St Mark's Square. A horn bellowed, scattering tourists and pigeons. Jake ran in pursuit. He wasn't the fastest runner and dared not raise too much suspicion by flying after the vehicle.

The hovervan turned out of sight around the Basilica. Frustrated, Jake teleported across the piazza. It was a short jump, and nobody appeared to notice despite the thunderclap that announced his arrival. He watched as the hovervan zoomed through the narrow streets, and out of sight once more. He dared not teleport again as he had no idea where he was going and could end up stuck in a wall, which meant certain death. Teleportation was also his only ticket away from Venice, and while he could use it to jump short distances, he needed a big enough 'charge' to get away.

Jake sprinted through the streets. The hovervan was heading straight for a canal. Now Jake realized why the Enforcers had chosen such an unusual mode of transport. The hovervan leapt off the jetty and splashed into the water. The air cushion bobbed it back above the surface and the vehicle shot along the canal.

If Jake didn't act fast he could easily lose the hovervan in the complex narrow system and although he knew the Hero Foundation had an outpost here, he didn't know *exactly* where. Time was against him.

Jake launched himself into the air and flew after the hovervan. He heard a gasp from a knot of tourists and there was a wave of camera flashes. No doubt the Enforcers would attempt to brainwash the tourists, convincing them that what they had seen was perfectly normal. They didn't seem to care about the consequences of scrambling people's minds.

The hovervan was more reckless than he was. A

gondola cutting across a junction was torn in half—the occupants leaping clear before the wooden boat was destroyed. Jake swooped around the corner so fast that his feet touched the building in front of him, forcing him to run along the vertical surface as he took the turn.

He was gaining on the hovervan. He hurled a lightning blast that dented the toughened roof of the vehicle—momentarily forcing it low into the water where it kicked up a spray that fogged Jake's vision.

When it cleared, there was a bridge in the way! Jake was flying too fast to avoid it. He had the fleeting glimpse of an astonished pedestrian's face before he slammed through the narrow stonework.

His shield absorbed the impact, preventing him from being splattered like a bug across the masonry. Centuries old stone cracked from the collision and he severed the bridge. As the footbridge collapsed into the water behind him, he spun wildly out of control—ricocheting between buildings either side of the narrow canal. Bricks crumpled and windows shattered as he pinballed.

Jake forced himself to a hovering stop to prevent further destruction. He had hoped that the theft of the equipment would go without a hitch—but as usual, things had gone wrong. Back in control, he shot after the hovervan as it turned another sharp corner.

New Kid on the Job

Jake easily caught up with the vehicle and fired another lightning blast that blew one of the doors open. Several crates of equipment spilled out, falling into the canal.

'Rats!' snarled Jake. Water-damaged equipment was no good to him. Jake surged forward—his fingers centimetres from grabbing the top of the vehicle. Then he became aware of two things simultaneously—a large motor yacht moored to the side of the canal on one side and a pair of fast approaching supers, flying on the other. Jake firmly gripped the top of the truck.

A pulse of energy suddenly struck the hovervan from the side—forcing it to veer into the moored yacht. Jake gripped tightly as he was yanked sideways. The vehicle hit the yacht with a loud crunch that echoed down the canal. The yacht acted as a ramp—forcing the hovervan to lift from the water. It rolled through the air. Jake spun with the van, riding it like a bucking bronco.

The hovervan barrel-rolled from the canal and landed on its roof in another smaller piazza filled with market stalls. Sparks kicked from the vehicle as it dragged across the concrete. They stung Jake's eyes and he let go.

A fruit stall cushioned Jake's fall. The broken hovervan rolled through several stalls before stopping. All around him, people screamed and ran for safety. Jake climbed unsteadily to his feet.

Two figures flew into the plaza—dressed, like he was, in casual clothing. It was a boy and a girl several years older than him.

'This catch is ours!' yelled the boy.

'No chance,' said Jake automatically. He was puzzled: if they were heroes why were they attacking their own delivery? Which could only mean they were villains. And Jake hated villains just as much as he despised heroes.

'Who's going to stop us, kid? You?' laughed the girl.

The two Enforcers climbed from the cab of the vehicle. They were badly beaten from the impact. The two new villains wasted no time in shooting both Enforcers with an energy blast that sent them sprawling through more stalls. Even Jake thought that was excessive force.

'Who are you?' asked Jake eyeing an unfamiliar logo on their sleeves. 'You know the Council has guidelines—' Jake couldn't believe he was telling somebody else off for breaking the rules.

'The Council of Evil are as antiquated as the Foundation,' snarled the boy. 'We're from Forge.'

The name meant nothing to Jake. He didn't want to get involved in a scrap—which showed how much he had matured since he had become the Dark Hunter. He preferred to find a sneaky way out of any situation he found himself in. Instead he resorted to the special weapon used by the rich and famous:

New Kid on the Job

'Do you know who I am?'

The teenagers looked at him blankly. Then the girl laughed. 'No, should we?'

Jake felt his cheeks burn from embarrassment. If you had to explain to somebody that you were famous, or infamous, then clearly you weren't.

'I'm the Dark Hunter!'

This got a reaction—a flicker of fear crossed both the teenagers' faces. Clearly they'd heard of his reputation.

'But you're only a kid,' said the girl.

Jake's temper snapped and he felt a surge of heat leave his finger. So much for the peaceful option! The lightning blast hit the girl like a sledgehammer. She hit the hovervan so hard that the metal dented and she slumped onto the ground, unconscious.

'NO!' screamed the boy and instinctively ran to the girl. It was an amateur mistake to turn his back on Jake. Jake fired a searing red fork of lightning at the boy. It sent him sprawling headfirst through a souvenir stall. Miniature porcelain gondolas broke over his head.

Jake stalked over to him. 'What's Forge?' The boy rolled over, gasping in pain. He stared defiantly at Jake. Jake gripped the boy's collar. 'I asked you a question!'

Jake suddenly felt a hail of needles shoot into the side of his face. The white-hot pain was unbelievable.

He dropped to his knees and turned to see that the girl's hands were a mass of spines like a porcupine. The ones she had fired at him were immediately replaced by more forming from her knuckles.

The next needle volley impacted into an energy shield Jake made appear around his arm. The speed of his manoeuvre surprised the girl.

Jake was losing his temper. He could feel the powers inside his body burn like fire.

Jake's vision tainted red and the girl appeared to glow as her body's electrical system became visible, highlighting her like an angel. He took some satisfaction in hearing her gasp as his eyes burned a menacing red.

Jake held out his hand and the girl became rigid. An invisible force hoisted her into the air and slowly crushed her body. She screamed.

'What is Forge?' yelled Jake.

She looked as though she was about to reply—but the boy suddenly swooped up and plucked her away. Jake fired wildly at them, blasting the rooftops of buildings as they disappeared behind them.

He could have followed them, but he needed to stay with the equipment. He took a deep breath and calmed himself. The redness in his vision bled away.

He looked around the trashed plaza, then to the van containing the Foundation's technology. At least he had accomplished the mission. All he had to do was teleport out with the merchandise and check Momentum was still alive.

Jake remembered being bored. Being bored was a sign of intelligence, so he had been told. It meant he wasn't doing enough to keep himself mentally active. Right now being bored sounded like a luxury.

He sat in his command centre, at the top of his castle's slender tower, and impatiently clicked the mouse button so hard that the plastic cracked under the pressure. He stared at the computer monitor, waiting for a satellite image to download.

Since he had been offered a seat on the Council of Evil, his life had been filled with pointless meetings and visits from sycophantic villains eager to make alliances with those in power. Most of the meetings consisted of the Council sitting around grumbling about how the Hero Foundation was continually foiling their plans. Other meetings involved listening to an assortment of bizarre, dangerous looking villains, all of whom had a plan to take countries over, steal precious items, kidnap key officials, and corrupt the world economy. And they were the saner ones. Most were denied permits to carry out their nefarious plans. Jake's old mentor, Basilisk, had told him that the permits were stifling creative villainy. In the good old days, villains could carry out their plans with impunity. Now they had to get permission from the Council so that they didn't accidentally disrupt another member's evil scheme.

It was pathetic. Jake marvelled at the fact that the Council was doing more to stem villainy than the Foundation was. If villains were free to carry out their plans, then the world would be in chaos. For every plan the Council allowed through, they earned a percentage of the ill-gotten gains. So it was no surprise they allowed more bank thefts through than plans to destroy the world.

Jake sat silently through these meetings, eager to leave the chamber. Like all Council members, Jake had been given quarters on his own private island that circled the main Council buildings. It was Chromosome's old set of offices and the biomechanical crud was still being cleaned off the walls. Jake preferred his own Gothic castle that Mr Grimm had given him.

Mr Grimm was a 'fixer', a double agent, working for both the Council and the Foundation in an attempt to maintain a balance between the two opposing forces. He had taken pity on Jake's unique situation and had gone out of his way to help him.

Jake felt Grimm was the only person he could really trust; especially after he had discovered his . . . girl-friend—the words still didn't sound right in his head—Lorna, was a hero, downloading her powers from Hero.com.

Jake enjoyed the isolation the castle provided. It was somewhere nobody could bother him as he spent several hours trying to watch his family through the Council's own surveillance satellites. The cameras were so powerful that he could zoom from the atmosphere, right down to read the headline of the newspaper tucked under his dad's arm.

When they were unable to see him, Jake had often sat with his parents in the house watching them live their lives without him. He had been a ghost. Since he had gone through all the trouble of obtaining Psych's superpower, his family could now see him, but not remember him. He had gone from ghost to stranger. That meant he could no longer sit with them and was forced to watch them from afar.

He watched his mum and dad cross the icy super-market car park and load the bags into the back of the car. It was another ordinary day, except his sister Beth wasn't with them. She hadn't been around for several days but his parents didn't seem too bothered by this. Jake guessed she was probably staying at a friend's house.

He watched the car pull away and his mind drifted. Momentum was still alive and well, and now in posses-sion of the Foundation gadgets they had stolen several days ago. He had won Momentum's trust by helping steal those gadgets.

He had searched the Council's database for 'Forge', but had drawn a blank. Even with the help of the Council's persistently happy artificially intelligent computer, Ernie, he had not been able to shed any light. Momentum was equally unaware of who they were.

With a sigh, he killed the satellite link and looked at his watch. It was time to meet Lorna in the hospital. Jake rubbed his temples; he was starting to get a headache. He had liked Lorna for ages, and she had helped him when he most needed it. They got on well together . . . until Jake had discovered she was a super-hero. Jake had been furious when Mr Grimm revealed this, but what could he do? He still liked her, and she didn't know *his* secret.

His headache got worse. Why wasn't life simple?

The Hero Foundation Hospital was a large modern building on the edge of a busy city. From the outside it looked like any other private institution, except inside it only dealt with superheroes wounded in the course of action. Raw healing powers, that resembled glowing slime, were drip fed to victims, enabling them to heal bones and even grow replacement organs and limbs.

There were always a couple of high-risk patients who

New Kid on the Job

could not be healed by traditional methods, usually victims of a previously unknown supervillain or they had been on the receiving end of a particularly nasty death ray.

Pete Kendall was one such patient. He was kept in a secure ward, linked to a life support machine that kept him alive through his coma.

Jake watched the bobbing line on Pete's machine. It was accompanied by a hypnotic beep. As usual, Lorna sat in the chair next to the bed and cried. Jake tried to act sympathetic, but the routine was becoming unbearable. He had tried to cheer Lorna up by giving her an expensive necklace he had stolen in a heist.

That plan hadn't worked and Lorna bombarded him with questions about where he had got it. In an effort to deflect her questions, he had told her it brought good luck and valued the necklace fifteen thousand pounds less than what it was worth. For some reason he couldn't fathom, she was happy it only cost a tenner.

'I could do with a drink,' said Jake after several minutes' standing in silence.

'I'll get it,' Lorna said and jumped to her feet. She left the room in search of a vending machine.

Jake smiled; he knew she'd do that. Lorna was still pretending to him that this was an ordinary hospital. She was doing everything she could to stop Jake snooping around and learning the truth.

Jake leapt into action. He had bypassed the Foundation's security with the help of Mr Grimm who managed to keep his presence a secret. Jake accessed the hospital via the roof, where Mr Grimm had conveniently deactivated the security.

Jake made sure the MP3 player, hidden under Pete's bed, was still working. As Momentum had said, it played a constant stream of subliminal messages that would wake Pete from the coma when a binary code phrase was spoken.

Jake sat back in his chair as Lorna reappeared with the drinks. He knew it wouldn't be much longer before he could wake Pete.

He stared at the comatose boy. The problem was, Jake had been bullying Pete at school for years, and he wouldn't welcome seeing him.

Jake knew that Pete would be woken from his coma using the subliminal pre-programming he and Momentum had been subjecting him to, then they had to break him from the Foundation's private hospital and convince him to join the Council of Evil. Only by making Pete his friend could Jake hope that the super would volunteer Psych's absorbed power and restore his family's memory.

Jake nodded. Then he would turn his full attention on bringing the Council of Evil to its knees.

It was a simple plan.

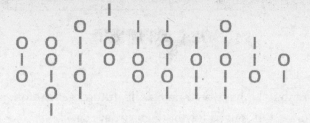

Unexpected Baggage

The air conditioning was making a reverberating grinding noise and doing nothing to cool the office. Amr Munir dabbed the sweat from his brow and stared at the computer screen with a sense of sadness.

The mouse pointer flicked through a series of photographs showing Munir in his glory days as a superhero called Blizzard. They had been times of great excitement and adventure as his team, the Justice Federation, battled evil across the world. He paused at one picture showing the whole team posing for the camera: Psych, Backdraught, and Hooded Harrier. Those were the days before the group had torn itself apart with constant bickering and now only Sandra Sinclair, aka the Hooded Harrier, and himself were still alive.

By the time Munir had turned forty, his superpowers had all but disappeared. Now he could only create a dribble of snow from his fingertips. He worked at

Istanbul University training the future generation of nurses, but longed for those glory days again.

He looked around his stuffy office. The walls were covered with certificates, all symbols of his great success. However, his chance encounter with a supervillain, Dark Hunter, had rekindled his adventure gene. Hunter was a Downloader, somebody who obtained their powers from the Internet rather than a Prime like him who was born with the natural gift.

During the Hero Foundation's last old-school reunion he had pleaded to be allowed to download powers from Hero.com so he could be a hero again, but their rules were strict. No Prime could download. When your powers ran out . . . that was the end of the line. Munir thought that wasn't fair: after all, there were still the lucky elderly Primes out there whose powers hadn't faded—the leader of the Hero Foundation, Commander Courage, for one. They would never experience the deep sense of loss Munir now felt.

Munir thought about Hunter, he hadn't seemed all that bad. More of a misguided kid than an absolute villain.

Maybe . . .

The idea suddenly struck him. If the Foundation was not willing to help him, then maybe Hunter would. After all, he had helped him locate Psych. Munir felt he was owed a favour.

Unexpected Baggage

Munir accessed a secret website. Perhaps he could find answers to his problems there.

Jake stood in the spacious entrance hall on Momentum's island. It had once been decorated with ornate support pillars, but Momentum had a habit of accidentally knocking them down, bringing portions of the ceiling with it. Now a complex carbon fibre trellis supported the roof. Jake thought it was tackily decorated, reflecting Momentum's baffling love of seventies music.

'Hunter!' called the big man as he entered the hall. He was smiling, which meant the consignment of gadgets Jake had stolen in Venice were still working. 'All systems go on my master plan!'

A thin, grey-haired man followed. He looked rather nervous and avoided eye contact with Jake.

'Are you going to share your plan with me?' Jake asked.

'No, it involves stopping Lord Eon from destroying the world with his time manipulation, so stop asking! There are plenty of forces involved in stopping him and we don't need your interference.'

Lord Eon had recently escaped from Diablo Island, and was currently pushing the world to a crisis point. The situation was so severe that both heroes and villains were fighting him.

Momentum continued. 'Needless to say, we both need the Kendall boy. He's nearly ready to be woken from his coma and escape from the Foundation Hospital and then he's yours.'

Jake stared at the weasely man. 'Who are you?'

'I'm called Simulacra.'

'What do you do?'

Simulacra shrugged. 'Stuff,' he mumbled.

'Leave him alone, he's with me,' said Momentum, placing a huge arm around Jake and gently guiding him away. 'Let's not question one-another's motives. I don't know why you need the boy and I don't care. You know how we are going to spring him out?'

'I read your briefing,' said Jake. Since joining the Council of Evil he had read more than he'd ever done at school. In fact he quite liked it. 'And after I've visited Pete again, are we ready to take our first Council member down?'

'The assassins are ready, as we planned, although it would help if I knew who you had marked for the first hit.'

It was Jake's turn to smile. 'I'm sure it would. You don't need to know yet.' Jake knew which of the Council members he wanted to get rid of first. It was the one who annoyed him most.

'As long as you're not going to double-cross me, then we should start this thing now.'

Unexpected Baggage

* * *

Jake walked from Momentum's chambers, his mind racing through a jumble of plans. He needed Momentum to help free Pete. Once he had Pete he didn't need Momentum, but would keep him around to help eliminate the other Council members. And once the Council was finished . . . then he could start on dismantling the Hero Foundation.

He crossed the slender bridge that connected Momentum's quarters to the main island that was bristling with hi-tech towers. This was the main hub of the Council's power where the technicians, administrators, and ambassadors lived. For them, working on an island of evil was just another job that paid well . . . if they remembered to keep their mouths shut.

Beneath him waves crashed and heavy rain pattered on the canopy above his head. He reached the far side of the bridge and a door, sporting Momentum's own rolling boulder logo, slid open. Jake walked through into the Council Chamber, trying to mentally walk through the plan he was about to unleash.

The chamber was circular and lit by dim red lights. Each of the Council members had a seat, of sorts, that circled the chamber. They were all empty now—the finest, most notorious villains were out concocting their diabolical plans.

Jake crossed to the exit—before he became aware that the chamber was not empty. A small figure was seated in an elegant chair, staring at him.

'Having an interesting conversation with Momentum were we?' It was a young girl's voice. Jake shivered as her words echoed around the chamber. It sounded as if a hundred people were whispering in the background of each word, and that wasn't anything to do with acoustics. The girl always sounded like that.

The figure lightly climbed from her throne and approached him. In the blood-red pools of light he could see her innocent face. She was about thirteen, with red hair tied in a ponytail. Her hands were folded inside her dungarees.

'That's my business,' said Jake brusquely, feeling a shiver go down his spine. While she looked like an innocent girl, and went by the name of Amy, he knew she was a genocidal maniac whose full title ran to: Amy: Yohg-Shuggor, the Destroyer of Worlds, the Bringer of the Night, the Spawn of the Damned, Eater of the Dead, the Apocalypse Harbinger, and the Shaker of Worlds.

Jake had no idea what all that meant but the other Council members genuinely feared her. He assumed she was some sort of anti-Christ, but then again he once thought his sister was too.

Amy didn't even try to hide the disdain in her eyes. 'I

Unexpected Baggage

don't like you, Hunter. I was against bringing you into the fold of the Council. We should have dissected you alive to see how you have become integrated into the V-net system.'

She was referring to the fact Basilisk had made Jake able to absorb powers from Villain.net because his own DNA was now part of the system. It had effectively made Jake addicted to the website. He needed to feed off the website every night to keep his strength up. He felt like a cyber-vampire. But the process did give him his unique ability to synthesize new and unseen powers. Rather than fight Jake for the secret held within him, the Council had decided to embrace him.

Jake matched her gaze with equal ferociousness.

'You're nothing but trouble,' she hissed, leaning close.

Jake smiled. That instantly angered Amy who was used to seeing her victims cower in fear.

'Oh, I *am* trouble,' agreed Jake. Then he turned his back on her and left. He took great satisfaction in hearing the snarls of rage that echoed around the chamber.

He was big trouble. She would find that out very soon. She was the first on his hit list.

As Jake walked across the manicured lawns of the Foundation Hospital, he felt his skin crawl and heard his bones crunch. His vision blurred momentarily as his

eyes changed shape and colour. By the time he had reached the range of the security cameras, he looked exactly like Lorna.

It was a cheap trick, and he hated doing it, but he'd spent so much time with Lorna that he knew he could replicate her accurately. He didn't want to rely on Mr Grimm to get him into the hospital. Grimm needed to be away from the events that were to unfold so that he didn't attract any undue attention.

The problem was that he could only control the power for several minutes. It was too much of a strain to hold it together for longer than that. He wondered how his shapeshifting arch-nemesis, Chameleon, managed it.

He walked unhindered through the hospital lobby. All around him biometric scanners analysed every visitor. He would be registered as Lorna. By the time he reached Pete's room, his face was burning up. He gently closed the door behind him and his skin snapped back into his regular appearance. He stung as if he had been slapped all over.

He stared at Pete, unconscious in the bed.

'Time to wake up, mate. You've got something I need.' Jake checked the subliminal MP3 player was still looping its hypnotic suggestions. 'If I didn't need it then I'd be quite happy to leave you to rot here and never see you again.'

Unexpected Baggage

He had hoped that he could simply extract the power from Pete's body, but Mr Grimm had told him it wasn't that simple. Pete's powers existed as fragments. They only came together when he willed it. In other words, Jake had to *be nice* to Pete. Pete must want to help Jake in order for the power to manifest. Jake hated the very thought of having to be nice to Pete.

Satisfied the subliminal message Momentum had developed was still working, Jake hit another button on the device. A high-pitched tone played. It was a series of binary code that Momentum had devised. It was designed to wake Pete once a key numerical sequence had been triggered by one of Momentum's agents— when Jake was safely out of the room. It was much safer than a keyword, such as 'attack', as there was no chance of Pete being woken before time. The binary tones interacted with Pete at a quantum level, ensuring that when he woke up, he would be in full control of his powers.

All Jake had to do now was ensure Pete woke in a bad mood so he would want to escape from the hospital.

Jake whispered close to his ear. 'That girl you like . . . Emily?' He glanced at the life support monitor. It spiked at the mention of her name. 'Emily . . . she's dead, you know?' Again the monitor spiked in response. *Somebody's still home*, thought Jake. Emily was a friend of Lorna's and it was obvious Pete had a crush on her—what a wimp. 'Your pal Toby killed her.' This provoked a fiercer response. Pete's fingers even clenched. 'He thought she was getting too big for her boots, so he decided to kill her and make it look like an accident.'

Jake felt oddly guilty about this misinformation. As far as he was aware, Emily was alive and well, but it was the best he and Mr Grimm could come up with to annoy Pete. Before he could spread any more malicious rumours the room door suddenly opened.

Jake spun round, red lightning crackling across his knuckles—he couldn't risk getting caught here in the heart of enemy territory. He was ready to fight his way out.

Lorna entered the room—her eyes immediately widening when she saw Jake standing ready to strike with electricity dancing from his fingers. Jake shot his hand behind his back—but it was too late, Lorna had seen him.

'Jake?'

'Lorna! I'm so glad to see you!' His mind was groping for a plausible excuse. He felt his cheeks flush red. 'Shut the door.'

Lorna closed the door and stared at Jake. 'You're a superhero? Like me! How long have you been . . . why didn't you say something?' She was flabbergasted. 'I can't believe you would keep something like this a secret from me! Don't you trust me?'

'Whoa, easy on the accusations! I've only just discovered about you . . . and what really happened to Pete.'

Lorna fell silent. Jake knew she had been desperate to tell him her secret, and now the cat was out of the bag.

She started to laugh and surprised Jake by giving him a quick hug. 'I'm so glad you know. I hated not saying anything. Why didn't Kirby or Grimm say anything?'

Eric Kirby was the founder of the Hero Foundation and worked closely with Grimm, unaware of his right-hand man's duplicitous nature.

'You know how tight security is around here.' Jake tried to sound casual, but he was coming to the realization that he couldn't let Lorna walk away with the knowledge of his powers. Mr Grimm had been sneaking him into the hospital under the noses of the Hero establishment. It was risky but necessary. The moment Lorna opened her mouth she would be told the truth about who Jake was: public enemy number one.

'What are you doing here?' he asked.

'I felt sick at school and asked to go home. Last night we were on a mission in Germany . . . and Emily vanished.' Jake caught sight of Pete's monitor reacting to Lorna's comment. 'We don't know where she is. After what happened with Pete, I'm starting to think none of this is worth the sacrifices we keep making. Why is life never easy?'

'Tell me about it.'

Lorna moved to Pete's side and watched him. 'How has he been?'

'The same,' said Jake with as much concern as he could muster. He had to get out. In a matter of hours the plan to spring Pete would unfold. He couldn't let anything stop it. 'We should really go.'

Lorna was absently playing with the necklace Jake had given her. 'Not yet, I've only just arrived.'

'I'm sure Pete'll be OK.'

Lorna stroked Pete's brow with one hand and twirled her long dark hair with the other. Jake knew her well enough to know that was a sign of deep thought.

'Didn't you say this necklace was lucky? Doesn't feel like it after last night.'

Jake sighed deeply, trying unsuccessfully to keep the desperation from his voice. 'Sure it is. We should go quickly. I'm on a mission.'

'I wanted to stay. I thought maybe talking to him would help break him out of the coma.'

'Why not give him the necklace? For luck? See if that works, but we have to go.'

'We?'

Unexpected Baggage

With a sinking feeling, Jake knew he was stuck with Lorna. 'Yes. I need your help.'

A smile flickered across Lorna's face. Jake felt sick. Was there anyone he wouldn't lie to and manipulate? He had thought that person was going to be Lorna . . . yet here he was. Lorna placed the necklace in Pete's limp hand.

'This is all my luck, Pete. You get through this. We all miss you.'

Jake wanted to vomit from all the sentimentality. He grabbed Lorna's hand and pulled her towards the door. But what was he going to do? He couldn't walk through the hospital because he would be recognized and Mr Grimm had warned him that if he teleported directly into the building alarms would be triggered. He had to get outside. He only had one option—the roof. It was the way Grimm had smuggled him in and out.

'Where are we going?' asked Lorna.

Jake looked long and hard at her. He really did want to tell the truth; maybe she would see that he was a victim of circumstance? He was forced to become a member of the Council of Evil and . . . of course she wouldn't believe him.

'Do you trust me?' He tried to sound joking.

Lorna frowned. 'Of course I do. Why?'

'You look a little pale. Sure you're OK? You're not going to faint, are you?'

Lorna shook her head and Jake touched her on the shoulder. He had been trying to muster the correct power and finally managed it.

For a second Lorna looked puzzled before a knock-out pulse shot through Jake's fingers and she slumped to the floor.

Jake sighed. He was beginning to think he was cursed with repetitive bad luck. He picked Lorna up and threw her over his shoulder. On the roof he could quantum tunnel away from the hospital before the sparks flew and Pete was freed.

The only question left was, what was he going to do with Lorna?

'Kill her.'

'Are you serious?'

'I'm always serious,' replied Mr Grimm. Jake couldn't argue against that. Mr Grimm adjusted his thin letter-box glasses and realigned his perfectly cut suit as he walked away from Lorna slumped unconscious in a chair. He examined several computer screens.

Jake had taken Lorna directly back to his castle in Transylvania, a base that Mr Grimm had given to him as a gift so they could conduct their plans in secrecy. They were in the uppermost tower that Jake had styled as his command centre. Lightning blasted outside, and

Unexpected Baggage

the rain drove harder against the glass—it was the perfect weather for his villainous lair.

'It's a perfect day for it,' commented Mr Grimm coolly. 'You shouldn't have brought her here.'

'I came back here for help. I couldn't exactly take her back to the Council. Dropping a hero right in the middle of their ultra-secret base, that wouldn't have gone down well.'

'She knows what you are.'

'She thinks I'm a hero.'

Mr Grimm shrugged his thin shoulders. 'And you think that disguise will stand up to even the most casual scrutiny? The moment she tells her brother or anybody else about you, the game is up. Killing her is the logical option.'

'I thought you were Mister Neutral? What happened to both sides having equal power?'

'Once you bring down the Council of Evil the Hero Foundation will quickly follow. That is balance. One extra dead superhero is nothing.'

'I thought you liked her?'

'I neither liked nor disliked. She was merely a tool for the job.' Jake thought that was a callous thing to say—and he was definitely no angel himself. 'If you don't want to do it, I'm sure Igor will oblige.' Igor was Jake's mute servant who, despite his name, was a good-looking six-foot man.

'Nobody is killing her.'

'Then she is your problem.' Grimm tapped the screen; it was showing an RSS news feed from Hero.com. 'It appears the plan worked perfectly. Momentum used a local businessman as his mind-controlled drone. He woke Pete at the right moment. It seems he fought with both Kirby and Toby before escaping. That was an unexpected bonus. Nobody will suspect who was really behind it all.'

'Excellent. Do we know where he went?'

'I'm picking up his CUCI.'

'What's a "cookie"?'

'It's an acronym for Cellular Uplink Communication Interface. The Foundation has recently created a genetic tag that is inserted into the wrist of every Downloader. It allows access to Hero.com, monitors vitals, and acts as a homing beacon. I took the liberty of extracting Pete's in the hospital and replacing it with one of our own so the Foundation won't be able to track him.'

'What about Lorna?' asked Jake in alarm.

'I took the liberty of jamming hers while she is here. Until you decide what you're going to do with her. She must not interfere with our plans to topple the Council. We have come too far to fail now. The first priority is Pete.'

'Remember, he's a priority so I can get my family

back. I don't care about what you and Momentum want me to do. The fall of the Council comes after my parents. Got that?'

Mr Grimm's lips tightened. He hated being talked down to by Jake, but knew better than to argue.

Jake looked pensive. 'So before we start hitting the Council members, you think I should talk to Pete?'

'The sooner you establish contact, the sooner you can win his trust. The moment you can convince him to create the anti-amnesiac power,' Grimm held up a small device that looked like a fat fountain pen, 'you use this sonic-extractor to pull it from him. The raw power fills the top of the device here, and then you reverse the switch and inject it into yourself. After that you will have no more use for him.'

'And I can use that power on my family.'

'Yes. They'll remember everything.'

Jake pocketed the sonic-extractor and looked across at Lorna who was still unconscious. 'Make sure she stays alive.'

'I'll ensure she remains unconscious.'

At least that means alive, thought Jake. Grimm handed him a slim locator that fixed on Pete's CUCI tag. The small display showed he was in a small village not too far from the hospital. It was time to go and say hello.

* * *

It was starting to snow and the girl could see her warm breath come out in rapid bursts of condensation. She forced herself to take longer, slower breaths; it helped combat the nerves. Despite the cold she was warm; she was physically primed for the mission and had been running off adrenalin since she left the Hero Foundation. Her stuffy facemask didn't help matters.

Through the trees she saw Dark Hunter and Pete Kendall standing in the field, quietly talking. From this distance they looked like any other kids, although Pete looked ill: his cracked skin was off-colour. There was no indication that they were two of the most powerful villains on the planet.

But she was ready for them. The Foundation had told her that her training was completely immersive. A week ago she had no idea that superpowers were real. Now she had been given a range of downloadable powers, all neatly available over a voice-activated headset. All she had to do was say the command and the power would be hers.

She watched as Pete walked away. Hunter glanced around—and she was certain he saw her. She backed away, twigs snapping underfoot. She froze as Hunter's head cocked. She blinked—and he was gone.

Dammit! A rookie mistake! After tracking Hunter all this time she couldn't afford to lose him now. Perhaps he had ducked down?

Unexpected Baggage

She suddenly sensed movement behind her and spun round.

Hunter was leaning against a tree, smiling quizzically.

'Let me guess, you've got some street name like Black Hawk or something?' He was clearly referring to her stylish charcoal body armour. 'Question is . . . which side are you on?'

'I'm bringing you in, Hunter.'

'You know my name. Fame at last! And where do you think you're taking me?'

'Diablo Island.'

Hunter cringed at the mention of the place he had been incarcerated in. Even though he had escaped, she saw a flicker of fear in his eyes.

'Look, kid, you can try and stop me and end up with a thousand bruises, if you're lucky . . . or dead if you're not. But it's your lucky day. I'm in no mood to fight.'

The girl summoned all her courage. This is what she had been trained for. She had seen the evil this villain had cast on the world. Even if he looked a few years older than her, she was going to do everything in her powers to complete the mission. She had been encouraged to hate Hunter.

And she really hated him.

She moved to attack—but Hunter was quicker. A

blue ball of flames from his hand shot a chunk from the tree behind her. The girl tensed and jumped nimbly halfway up a tree. Hunter fired again, blowing dry branches apart as she sprang from tree to tree much faster than he could follow.

The girl had super-dexterity. She had trained for days in a simulator room. There was no way she was going to allow herself to be hit by Hunter's clumsy shots.

He was relying on brute force. She was a surgical instrument.

Hunter's last fireball caused the tree boughs to erupt into flame above his head. Hot cinders rained down on him, stinging his eyes.

It was just the distraction the girl was looking for. She jumped in front of him and launched an energy sphere that enveloped him.

Hunter was dragged backwards, inside the sphere—crashing through trees with such force that several were split in two. Rather than protect him, the energy sphere amplified the impact.

Seconds later the ball disappeared and he was thrown against a broad oak trunk. He slid to the ground, feeling more pummelled than he had for a long time. The girl glided over to him, ready to deliver another attack—but Hunter was playing possum—

As the girl landed in front of him he punched her stomach and discharged a lightning blast. He had never fired one while still touching his target—and now he knew why.

Hunter's entire body shook as though he was shooting himself. The blast lifted both the girl and the arch-villain off their feet and flung them apart. For several metres they both bounced off trees. Jake landed on his feet, but the girl was worse for wear. The front of her uniform was buckled and smoking. The carbon-fibre weave resembled melted plastic. The landing impact had knocked her facemask off.

Hunter ran to her, intending to finish the hero off. He raised his hand for the final blow . . . then hesitated.

He recognized the pale, bloodied face. The girl's long blonde hair, which had been tied in a neat ponytail, was everywhere and covered in twigs and brown leaves. She glared at him.

'What you staring at?'

'Beth?'

'You think you know me?'

Hunter was stunned. 'Beth? You're . . . you're my *sister*!'

Beth Hunter smiled. There was no humour in it.

'They told me you'd try that one.'

Then she shot her brother in the face.

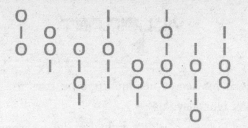

Sibling Rivalry

Lorna awoke with a stabbing headache. Her vision swam, making her feel dizzy. When it finally became clear she bolted upright. She was lying in a large bed, in an elegant stonewalled room. A large window was blurred with heavy rain and all she could tell was that it was dark.

She climbed from bed, feeling a little weak. A large oak door suddenly opened and a tall handsome man entered carrying a tray. On it was a bowl of soup.

'Hi,' said Lorna. 'Er . . . where am I?'

The man simply smiled and laid the tray on a table.

'Are you not allowed to talk to me?'

'Igor is mute,' said Mr Grimm striding into the room. Lorna was surprised to see him, but at least she felt comforted by the familiar, if emotionless, face. 'He is Hun . . . Jake's servant and will get you anything you need.'

'Jake's servant?' asked Lorna in disbelief. 'You mean all of this is Jake's?'

'This is his secret headquarters he uses for critical missions. Igor, leave us.'

'Wow!' Lorna couldn't help but be impressed. All she, Toby, Emily, and Pete had ever received for risking their lives to be heroes was a pat on the back. Jake must be important to get all this. 'Is he rich?' She couldn't stop the question tumbling from her mouth.

'Very. He is not here at the moment. He's taking care of business. In the meantime make yourself at home, but please don't wander around. There are areas of the castle that are . . . dangerous.'

'Castle . . . this is so cool!' Then a sobering thought brought reality back. 'What happened in the hospital? The last thing I remember was speaking to Jake . . . then I must have fallen unconscious.'

'You were attacked by Pete. Jake saved you and brought you here to keep you safe.'

Lorna frowned. She had no recollection of this. 'Why would Pete attack me?'

'He awoke from his coma with a very different outlook on life. But do not concern yourself, that isn't important. The Foundation are dealing with it as we speak.'

'Is he OK?'

'That remains to be seen.'

'And Emily? Is she still missing?'

'We know where she is. And she is alive. Again, do

not worry. Measures are being taken to retrieve her and neutralize that particular threat.'

'What does—'

'I don't have time for questions, Lorna,' Grimm snapped. 'Jake will be back soon with *answers.*' He sucked in his breath, calming down. 'Perhaps you should rest a bit more. That often clears the mind.'

Mr Grimm left after a curt goodbye. Lorna was still wondering how important Jake must be to have succeeded in getting a place like this. It certainly explained his long absence from school.

Then there was Pete. He was really a friend of her brother's, but they had become close when they discovered Hero.com and had been plunged into a world of danger.

She had cried over Pete while he had been in a coma. And now he had apparently attacked her, she was torn between never wanting to speak to him again, and a wave of sympathy. Absorbing so many raw superpowers must be affecting his judgement. She refused to believe Pete, of all people, could turn bad.

She ate the soup and allowed herself a rare moment to relax. She didn't hear another sound except the incessant rain battering the window.

After thirty minutes, boredom had started to creep in. Grimm had told her it was dangerous to wander around, but she was capable of taking care of herself.

She checked her touch screen phone—it had no signal.
The phone was a gift from the Foundation and allowed
her to access Hero.com and download powers at any
time. Luckily it stored a batch of 'micro-powers'—
short, sharp dosages of the last dozen powers she had
downloaded, that would last for seconds. It was a little
like a web browser's 'history' function. Even if the
micro-powers lasted for seconds, it was usually enough
to get out of a tricky situation.

Lorna opened the door and looked around the wide
Gothic hallway.

'Hello? Igor?'

Her voice echoed and remained unanswered.
She decided to explore a little. Most rooms she
encountered were locked and she didn't think it was
polite to kick them open. Other rooms were completely bare.

She reached a spiral staircase. A steel door with an
electronic access panel blocked the way up. Obviously
something important lay beyond. Lorna decided to
descend the stairs.

The steps ended in a large entrance hall. Her trainers
sank into a carpet so soft it was like walking on moss.
Again all the doors were locked. Now she was starting
to feel frustrated. Why all the secrecy?

A set of double doors caught her attention. She
peered through the keyhole. Her narrow field of vision

revealed a comfortable looking lounge with a blazing log fire on one wall, and more importantly, a TV.

She checked her phone again and was annoyed to see it still had no reception. Then she remembered a power she had used a few weeks ago that could be useful now.

She accessed the stored bank of micro-powers on the phone and found it—the last one on the list. She double-tapped it.

The phone screen pulsed as the powers transferred— it was part of Hero.com v2, a much faster and cleaner method than the probing finger that used to warp out of the screen.

With the power tingling in her hand she pushed her finger against the lock. Her fingertip extended into the keyhole and ran along the pins. It morphed until it perfectly matched the key-shape like a skeleton key. Then she twisted her finger and the door unlocked—seconds later she felt the power fading from her system. She checked the phone, and sure enough, the skeleton-key power had disappeared from there too. She hoped she wouldn't need it again.

She swung the double-doors open and entered the spacious living room. She was sure Jake wouldn't mind. She sat on the couch and found the remote control resting on the table.

A news channel was playing a story about an unusual storm that had battered a village in Ireland. She flicked through the channels to something more entertaining—then became aware that she wasn't the only person in the room.

She looked at the figure in the corner—and gasped in astonishment.

Jake sprinted through the woods. Tree branches whipped at his face. He only had one good eye, the other was pulped, and it felt gooey, clinging to the mutilated flesh on the side of his face. If Beth's shot had been on target then Jake was certain he would have died.

With just one eye his depth perception was gone. He stumbled several times to his knees; only the sound of Beth pursuing kept him going.

The trees gave way to a farm. Jake jumped a small wooden fence and ducked around a red-brick outbuilding. He darted across a muddy track and hid in a barn.

He pressed himself up against a tractor and concentrated on battling the pain that pulsed through him. His regeneration powers were gradually kicking in and the side of his face, which looked like a deflated soccer ball, was slowly reforming. He had to focus hard not to fall unconscious from the pain.

Through the slits in the barn walls he saw Beth slowly pass. He was amazed that the Hero Foundation had recruited her. Of course she now had no memory of who he was—to her he was a stranger, a member of the Council of Evil, the ultimate enemy. How could he possibly attack his own sister? The plan was diabolically brilliant. The founder of the Hero Foundation, Eric Kirby, would make a despicable villain.

As his face healed, Jake readied himself to quantum tunnel away from the farm. Nothing happened. The shimmering portal that he willed to open in the air failed to materialize.

Beth's voice echoed across the farm. 'You're not getting away from me, Hunter! I've got a device that nullifies your ability to teleport, tunnel, or fly out of here.'

Jake was worried. He tried to fly up to the barn rafters but found he couldn't. He looked around for anything that would help him escape. The barn was filled with a variety of sharp spiky ploughing implements. There was nothing useful there.

'You have to face the Reaper.'

Despite the tenseness of the situation, Jake couldn't stop himself laughing. Since he had been separated from his family, his sister had been listening to his IronFist MP3s. She had taken her pseudonym from one of their tracks.

The barn door suddenly exploded into matchsticks. Beth stood in the doorway, energy crackling in her hands. She must have heard him laugh.

He ducked behind the tractor. 'I don't want to fight you, Beth!'

'Too bad, you're going to have to. Unless you come peacefully, of course, but I don't believe that's your style.'

'Beth, listen to me. I am your brother. The Foundation wiped your mind of my existence, that's why you can't remember me.'

'Forget the mind games, Hunter. I've been warned about you.'

She extended a hand and the tractor suddenly rose into the air, hovering in the rafters and exposing Jake. Jake climbed to his feet and raised his hands to calm her.

'Whatever they told you is a lie!'

'You're part of the Council of Evil, responsible for kidnapping, blackmailing world leaders, destroying the Statue of Liberty, the Sydney Opera House, Air Force One, and kidnapping the President of the United States—'

'OK, OK . . . I admit I've done a few things wrong. But if I'm lying to you, if I'm really that bad, then why aren't I attacking you?'

'Because you're afraid of me.'

'Afraid of you?' Jake couldn't keep the sarcasm from his voice.

Beth scowled. Jake knew she never had much

Sibling Rivalry

patience with him when she remembered him. Her attitude was a sign that some things obviously were not completely forgotten. She slammed the tractor down on Jake. He dived to safety at the very last second—but was hit as one of the oversized rear tyres sheared from the axle and knocked him to the floor.

Jake reacted instinctively—and seized some nearby ploughing equipment with telekinetic force. Beth ducked and the heavy five-blade furrow plough tore through the wall behind her, but she wasn't lucky enough to avoid the multiple scythe-like blades of a cultivator. She dropped to the floor and screamed loudly as a blade severed her hand! There wasn't much blood as her healing factor immediately sealed the wound—but she felt the pain.

The scream was enough to pull Jake back to reality. He had let his anger control his actions with no thought of the consequences. He reined back the fury he felt bubbling under his skin. He couldn't afford to unleash his full powers on his sister.

'Beth! I'm sorry!'

She was clutching her stump, tears pouring down her cheeks. She dragged her gaze from her hand on the floor and shouted at Jake.

'It's not growing back!' she wailed.

Jake didn't know what to say. He'd had many

wounds in the past, but never a missing limb. He was unsure if any healing factor could cure that level of injury. He was staring at Beth's twitching hand—he didn't see her raise her stump.

A burst of power blasted Jake off his feet. He struck another piece of machinery—an overturned seed tiller. The plethora of wicked blades punctured his body, sucking the breath from him.

He gasped as his regeneration power healed the wounds, effectively sealing around the blades poking from his chest and arms. Beth approached him, still crying as she held her stump across her chest.

'They wanted me to bring you in alive. But you don't deserve that privilege!'

Jake tried to move, but the blades were holding him tight. After all the supervillains and heroes he had fought, he found it inconceivable that he was about to die by the hands of his amnesiac sister. The very sister whose memory he was trying to restore so she could lead a normal life once more.

'Beth, don't do this,' pleaded Jake. 'I know how to restore your memory. I can help you . . . Mum and Dad—'

'Shut up about my parents! You don't know them!'

'Our parents! Do you remember when we were on holiday in Spain and you fell off that donkey? And Dad—'

Sibling Rivalry

'I remember it. I remember that you were *not* there. Stop trying to read my mind, Hunter.'

'I'm not!' Jake was exasperated.

Beth examined her stump. She obviously thought Jake was no longer a threat now he was trapped. She forgot he was much more experienced at the super-power game. He didn't need his hands to strike back.

Jake squinted; his eyes momentarily became completely red as his power kicked in. He had no conscious idea what superpower he was going to create, only the desired result. Jake willed the air molecules in front of Beth to pack so tight that they became solid. An invisible hammer punch threw Beth across the barn.

Jake didn't waste any time in gloating. He blinked, his eyes changing colour from red to pure black. He couldn't feel the heat himself, but a stream of microwaves pulsed from his eyes. As he stared at the metal spars protruding through his body, they melted like wax. He slid himself off the machinery, his healing factor rapidly mending him.

Beth was scrambling to her feet. Jake had no intention of hanging around. He blasted a hole through the barn wall and dived through.

Jake sprinted across an icy yard that was bordered by a large farmhouse. He was looking for any means of escape—what he wasn't expecting to see was an angry farmer coming out of the house with a pump-action shotgun. 'What you doing trespassin'? You hoodie!'

Jake skidded low as the barrels exploded in his direction. The pellets bounced from a shield that appeared in front of Jake a nano-second later. The farmer quickly re-aimed. Jake raised his hands and blindly shot a fireball at the man. He didn't pause to watch the farmer get thrown back into his house.

An energy blast destroyed a section of wall near his head. Jake didn't bother turning round. Beth was coming. He ran towards a cylindrical grain silo that stood in the far corner of the farm. Another power-volley chewed the ground close by. He was glad that his sister was a terrible shot.

He had to get away from her. Whatever device she used to nullify his powers must have a maximum radius. Beyond that, he could teleport out of danger.

Another energy blast flew over his head and tore a concrete chunk from the wall of the silo halfway up. Fine grain cascaded out. Jake was forced to run through it and started coughing from the cloud of fine dust that was being kicked up.

He reasoned that a barrage of warning shots might prevent Beth from following him so eagerly. He summoned a fireball into the palm of his hand. It was too small to do any real damage, but it would hopefully scare her.

Sibling Rivalry

'Hunter! No!' Beth screamed.

Jake watched as the bright orange ball leapt from the palm of his hand. He suddenly vaguely recalled a science teacher telling the class about how fine particles can be explosive—but, as usual, he hadn't really listened. One second later the entire grain silo exploded with devastating ferocity.

The top quarter of the tower shot directly up like a rocket. The rest of the structure blossomed outwards in a magnificent orange fireball, shattering every window on the farm, tearing slates off roofs, and toppling several outbuildings.

Jake felt his skin burn as a pressure wave tossed him three hundred metres. He felt himself bounce off a rooftop, and he spun wildly before crunching into the ground. Half his bones had broken. Jake lay there, pelted by debris that continued to fall from the sky long after his bones had healed and cracked back into place.

When he could finally look up he saw that the farm was devastated. Half the house had been torn down, and a Land Rover in the driveway had been thrown into an adjacent field.

'Beth?' Jake yelled, getting to his feet. Could his sister survive such an explosion? Had he killed her? Guilt made his stomach burn, and he felt his legs shake. He tried to fly to obtain a bird's-eye view, but found his power was still being jammed. That meant Beth's device was active, not necessarily that she was alive.

The snowstorm was increasing as Jake dropped to his knees. He had killed his sister . . . that was unpardonable. The wind picked up, suddenly as strong as a tornado. Jake looked up to see an elderly helicopter landing close by.

A figure ran from the chopper towards him. It was probably an Enforcer. If so he didn't care any more. He'd let them take him.

'Jake Hunter!' yelled a man over the roar of the rotors.

Jake looked up, wiping a stray tear from his eye. The man was strangely familiar.

'Hunter! Come with me, I'll get you out of here!' Jake was confused and hesitated before taking the man's outstretched hand. 'We don't have much time. She's down, but not out. I saw her from the air.'

Jake felt a sudden wave of optimism. 'She's alive?'

The man was nervous. 'Very much so, and her jammer will prevent you from leaving here, unless we go by more traditional means.' He jerked a thumb towards the helicopter.

Jake followed. His emotions were a delicate seesaw. He was delighted she was still alive—but he had no desire to run into his sister again. As soon as they climbed aboard, the man adjusted the collective and the machine rose smoothly into the air.

Sibling Rivalry

The destruction looked far worse from the air. Dozens of trees close to the silo had been flattened in a circular pattern around the explosion. The falling snow made it difficult to define details—but Jake caught sight of a black clad figure pushing masonry off herself.

His sister was alive. He hoped she could reattach the hand—if she could find it amongst the debris. That thought squashed his elation—he had been responsible for chopping her hand off.

What a terrible brother he was.

Jake was weary from wrestling with his conscience. Instead he turned his attention to his saviour. He knew him, but couldn't remember from where.

'We've met before haven't we?' said Jake.

The man smiled. 'Indeed we have. I helped you out once before. I think this makes it twice. My name is Amr Munir.'

It all came back to Jake and he nodded.

'I see you remember. Good. I've been looking for you, Hunter. I want you to restore my powers.'

'How?'

'Through Villain.net.'

'But you're a hero.'

'Not any more. The Foundation sampled my powers to synthesize, and then they abandoned me when my gifts faded. You can restore them. I want to be your *sidekick*.'

Sidekick

Lorna ran her fingers over the smooth opaque surface of the statue. The detail was so precise that there was no getting away from it—it had to be real. She had found one of the Foundation's top operatives who was listed as Missing in Action: Chameleon.

What was he doing here? She tried to move the statue but it was heavy. Her foot crunched small stones littering the base. She didn't dare break the crystalline case—she'd had an experience in Germany when she'd seen several crystallized villains shatter. It wasn't a pretty sight.

'Chameleon? Can you hear me?'

If he could, there was no way he could respond. Lorna pulled out her phone. She had to alert the Hero Foundation that she'd found him . . . then she hesitated.

Surely the Foundation knew Jake had found Chameleon? With no phone reception she couldn't call anybody to check. She tapped the amber casing; there was no way to break it open.

If Jake was already on the way back with a team of technicians to free Chameleon, then he might not be happy that she had broken into the room and interfered with his rescue mission.

Lorna sat back down on the couch and stared at the statue. She was torn between duty and respect for Jake.

There was no doubt in her mind that if Jake had found Chameleon then he was the hero of the hour.

She didn't doubt him in the slightest.

Jake knew that he shouldn't bring a member of the Hero Foundation to the Council of Evil. Both sides fiercely protected the secrecy of their locations and to walk straight in with the enemy was a stupid thing to do.

However, Jake was never one to play by the rules. Munir may have once been a hero, but now his powers were all but gone. Jake didn't think he was any kind of threat. The only other alternative was to take Munir to his own castle lair, but Lorna had been there since last night. He didn't think it wise to introduce the two heroes, especially since Lorna thought he was on her side. He didn't want to think about what he was going to do with Lorna; that was a headache for another time.

Munir had landed the chopper several miles from

the farm. They abandoned it on a school playing field and Jake teleported them both to his private chambers at the Council.

Mr Grimm's face was a mask of rage when Jake turned up with Munir. The hero immediately recognized him.

'Grimm? What are you doing here?'

'Why the hell is he with you?' screamed Mr Grimm. Jake was taken aback by the rare display of emotion Grimm was showing. 'He knows who I am!'

'He wants to defect,' said Jake.

Munir smiled calculatingly. 'So you're a traitor?'

'I work for my own interests, Blizzard. And if you wish to defect, it is you who is betraying the values and morals you once held so dear.'

Munir scowled. 'The Foundation used me and spat me out. As well you know. You were once a part of that process.'

'You were an asset. And assets only have a limited shelf life.'

Jake looked at Mr Grimm quizzically. Did that comment apply to him too? Grimm didn't notice. He was glaring spitefully at Munir.

Munir shrugged. 'Which is why I'm here. I want those glory days back, I want to download powers from Villain.net. I have helped Hunter twice now, so in return I ask this favour.'

'Hunter. A word please,' Mr Grimm said.

'Go ahead.'

'In *private*.'

Grimm strode from the room. Jake felt his cheeks flush. It was like the headmaster telling him off. He didn't have to put up with that! He was one of the most powerful supervillains on the planet!

Jake angrily followed Grimm.

In a separate, soundproof room, Grimm was trying to control his anger.

'Are you deliberately trying to sabotage our plans? Munir can tell the Foundation everything about us! Where you live . . . my involvement!'

'He saved me. I think I owe him this chance.'

'You owe him nothing!'

'Did you know the Foundation had recruited my sister? They have trained her up to come after me.'

'Ah, Reaper. Yes. I was told what happened.'

'Oh, so you do know? I'm really glad you told me!' snapped Jake. 'Don't you dare have a go at me when you're keeping secrets like that!'

'I had no idea Reaper was your sister! The Foundation had formed a secret operation to capture you, and Reaper was the codename. The asset was to be given powers from Hero.com and intensive training. The project was classified beyond my access level. It was only known to a select few. To use your sister . . . is a stroke of genius.'

'I'm glad you're so happy for them,' growled Jake. 'She almost killed me out there and it was Munir who saved me. She has some kind of device that prevented me from teleporting away.'

'Yes, a snag-net. Since the near destruction of the Foundation by your old friend Basilisk, they have been upgrading their systems. The snag-net is a prototype device that uses a raw nullifying power to prevent any forms of transport. Once you are in close proximity you won't be getting out in a hurry. But you did escape and you broke protocol by bringing a hero here. What are you thinking? And you took Lorna to the castle; are you going to invite every waif and stray?'

'I couldn't leave Lorna in the hospital because she would have told them that I had been there—and then she would know I'm no hero. I had no choice!'

'You're becoming sloppy, Hunter. You have lost your edge since joining the Council.'

Jake backhanded Grimm across the face. He knew he shouldn't have: Grimm had shown him nothing but understanding and sympathy since they had met. It was the bully inside Jake that forced his hand. Grimm reeled back with a bloody lip, and looked at Jake in astonishment. For a second Grimm's face wavered and Jake caught sight of the skull face that gave Grimm his name. Jake took a deep breath—the art of bullying was to make sure your victims cowered before you.

'Don't talk to me like some kid,' Jake retorted. 'Remember who you're dealing with. Remember what I'm capable of!'

Mr Grimm held his anger in check. 'Of course, Hunter. I am aware of this, I only worry that your emotions are clouding your decisions. Munir shouldn't be here.'

'He wants to be my sidekick.'

'Sidekick? You don't need one. Only weak heroes take on sidekicks.'

'Then he's my henchman. Whatever you want to call it, I think it will be good having him around.'

'And if he betrays us?'

'He won't. He hates the Foundation and he did help me find Psych, and saved my neck from my sister back there.'

'So you want to hook him up to Villain.net and see what happens?'

'What harm can it do?'

'You are a product of the harm it can do to tinker with the V-net system. The Kendall boy is another example of what happens when these powers are misused. You saw his skin, off-coloured and crumbling. It's breaking up at a molecular level, and only his internal healing power is holding him together. Nobody has switched from Hero.com to Villain.net, especially one so old . . . and a Prime. All these factors could spell disaster.'

A dull chime echoed through the chamber—the Council were being summoned.

'Look on the bright side,' said Jake. 'If it kills him, you'll have got your way.'

Grimm shook his head. 'It's just another distraction from the plan. We went through a lot to get you on the Council and we can only destroy it from the inside out.'

'It's not a distraction. I'm going to deal with our first target now.' Another dull chime reverberated. Jake headed for the door. 'You hook up Munir to Villain.net and get him ready. I may need some back-up.'

One of the many ambassadors who ensured the Council of Evil ran smoothly, escorted Jake to his alcove in the circular Council chamber. Jake's eyes were still adjusting to the dim red light. By the time he sat on his plush throne, he could make out the other alcoves.

Directly opposite sat Amy; her narrow eyes never left him. She had hated him from the very moment he had been recruited. In the alcove next to her was Momentum. The big man never looked at Jake. In the chamber they deliberately avoided conversation, giving the impression that they were enemies when in fact they had organized their plan to destroy the Council with Mr Grimm right down to the finest detail.

Another pair of sinister Council members, Professor Mobius and Fallout, sat along from Momentum. The two were in quiet discussion. Mobius possessed psychic abilities and Jake often worried the fiend knew what he was scheming.

A splashing noise to Jake's right caused him to look over. The alcove was filled with a steaming jacuzzi that had been empty when Jake walked past. Now the water surface rippled and a humanoid form rose from it—he was Abyssal. Jake guessed there must be a pipeline that connected Abyssal's seat at the Council to the surrounding ocean. The villain's voice started like a kettle whistle then settled into a gargle.

'I heard about your sister, Hunter.' Abyssal gave a gentle laugh.

'You find it amusing?'

'The Foundation tore your family apart, turned your best friend on to you and now this. It's enough to make you wonder who the true villains are. Us or them.'

Jake couldn't agree more.

The last two members entered the chamber side-by-side, which was unusual since it was a well known fact they mistrusted one another.

The first was Armageddon, a powerfully built villain

who suited his name perfectly. Black armour clung to him and seemed to absorb the shadows. He had four muscular arms and his head was distorted so that it fanned out at the crown, reminding Jake of a triceratops dinosaur. He was openly supportive of Jake's appointment and acted as if they were old friends. Mr Grimm had warned Jake of the old Mafia saying: keep your friends close, and your enemies closer.

The second figure was Necros—a lanky man draped in darkness. A torn cape hung from his shoulders and a rusty crown sat on his head. He was the leader of the Council, even though the Council officially had no leader and all decisions were supposed to be made collectively. The problem was that Necros was the most powerful of them all and nobody dared challenge him. The last person who tried was Chromosome and she had paid for the treachery with her life.

Jake knew that he couldn't start by toppling Necros. There were too many members of the Council who would be willing to join their leader in a fight—because if Necros won they didn't want it to look as though they had stood around and watched the fight with glee. Jake knew he couldn't fight those odds. He would have to play a waiting game, making sure everybody else was out of the picture before he faced Necros.

'Let the Council session begin,' boomed Necros in a sonorous voice.

Jake settled back in his chair. He would have to go through all the rubbish business before the action began. When he looked at Amy he tried to keep the smile from his face. He would enjoy watching her fall.

The War Room was a brand new construction for the Hero Foundation. It was located in the heart of the New Mexico desert in America and was designed to train heroes up to face the most intensive action. In a room the size of a football field, hundreds of machines would fire a vast variety of weapons at a hero in training. Knives, arrows, poison, acid, and bullets were all common assault weapons—all designed to give a hero real-world experience.

The greatest creation was the Nebulous—a series of Artificially Intelligent robot drones that tapped into Hero.com and simulated attacks using superpowers. They acted as a hive mind, sharing information and working together to complete their missions. By altering various power combinations they could simulate almost any supervillain, or supervillain team, in the world.

Eric Kirby, the leader of the Hero Foundation, stood behind a protective screen watching as a young hero dodged the attacks below. The hero was not quick enough for the Nebulous—two drones blasted him to the floor in a pincer attack.

Sidekick

With the hero down an alarm sounded and the room reset. The drones' weapons powered down and they returned to recesses around the room where they were sealed in by thick blast doors. A team of medics ran into the room to tend to the unconscious hero.

Kirby sighed. The latest batch of recruits was turning out to be rather clumsy and slow. They may have restored the integrity of Hero.com, but the Foundation lacked foot soldiers.

The door behind him opened and Beth walked in. She looked gloomy.

'Beth, my dear, how are you feeling?' Kirby asked in a happier voice than he really felt.

'Awful,' she said, staring at her left arm that was held in a sling against her chest. It was still handless.

'We are continuing to search the site, but it seems increasingly obvious that your hand was destroyed in the blast,' said Kirby. He felt a wave of guilt for the lie. They *had* found Beth's hand, and could have re-attached it, but Kirby had decided that the missing appendage would fuel Beth's hatred towards Hunter. It would be a small price to pay for bringing in the Dark Hunter. And afterwards they should be able to reattach the cryogenically frozen hand.

Beth stared at the stump. 'I'm going to get him for this.'

'Good. That's exactly what we want you to do.'

'Do you know where he is? I don't feel like waiting for revenge.'

Kirby was impressed with the venom in her voice. He shook his head. 'He's gone to ground, no doubt frightened by your attack. However, we have agents in the field monitoring him. As soon as he raises his head—he's all yours.'

In fact the news Kirby had received was very encouraging. It distracted him from the immense problems they were facing with the time controlling maniac, Lord Eon, who was close to throwing the world into chaos. Beth was the only resource he could spare to find Hunter—but now he had a mole inside Hunter's organization. It hadn't been planned and was an unexpected coup.

'Why don't you do a little more training in the meantime?'

'I've trained enough,' growled Beth.

'Not with that injury you haven't. Try some psychokinetic powers to help you cope. They will be more effective than a hand.'

Beth reluctantly left the room. Kirby gazed at the door long after it had closed. On the surface Beth was the complete opposite of her brother, but as her training scratched away the veneer of manners and niceness, it seemed they were both the same at the core.

He would have to make sure Reaper was kept in check. The Foundation didn't need any more rogue agents like Pete Kendall.

Mr Grimm watched as Munir's body convulsed on the table. A team of Council scientists flocked around him, monitoring his vital signs. While most of the scientists came from normal everyday back-grounds, a couple sported wild hair and manic grins that had earned them the collective tag of 'the Mad Scientists'. Some even wore a team T-shirt with the slogan on.

Villain.net was projected on a large holographic screen. Grimm watched as the scientists administered small doses of power into the Prime. Munir's body reacted violently as a flight power was downloaded, straight from the digitizing server, down a wire, and into his arm. He screamed out.

Mr Grimm stood inside a control room; a thick screen protected him from any accidents inside the download chamber. He still winced though when Munir's screams played over the speakers.

'How much more of this can he bear?' Grimm asked the computer terminal.

The chipper voice of Ernie, the Council's artificially intelligent computer system, spoke: 'His pain threshold is incredibly high. A normal subject would have passed out minutes ago.'

Grimm hated Ernie's voice and made a mental note to have it changed to a more formal one when addressing him.

'They're ready to administer Blizzard's original powers,' said Ernie cheerfully.

Grimm watched as the mad scientists used the new computer system to drag the icons from one screen and place them together on another that displayed what was about to be pumped into Munir.

The powers had been stolen from the Hero Foundation, so would presumably be clones of the ones Munir had donated. Inserting them back into the host was something that had never been attempted before.

The scientists took a cautious step backwards from the ex-hero as the powers downloaded. Mr Grimm couldn't help but notice two of the scientists were crouching behind machinery as though they expected Munir to explode.

Munir shuddered on the table as the powers were forced into his body.

Grimm turned down the volume control so he didn't have to continue listening to Munir's high-pitched wailing.

* * *

Sidekick

Jake wondered if he had nodded off during Professor Mobius's round up of the Council's financial gains during the last spate of dastardly activity. His sibilant voice echoed around the chamber and he seemed to stutter on the esses.

During the Hero Foundation's recent troubles, the Council had issued more warrants to supervillains than ever before, and since the Council took a ten per cent fee from any villainous loot plundered, they had done exceptionally well with over two hundred million dollars in one month. Mobius was even suggesting that the villain who obtained the most cash in any given year should be awarded some sort of 'employee of the month' prize.

Jake sniggered. He could imagine an award for 'the most cunning plan', another for 'most victims maimed'.

'Any other business before we retire?' Necros asked.

Jake looked around. The other members he could see all looked as bored as he did. He needed to keep the Council assembled for a few more minutes. He suddenly remembered something that had been nagging him since Venice.

'I do.'

'Dark Hunter has a question for the Council,' barked a small ambassador, whose job it seemed was only to repeat anything anybody else said.

'Who or what is "Forge"?'

He noticed Armageddon lean forward in his chair. A couple of other Council members reacted to the name too.

'How did you come by this name?' asked Necros.

Jake was intrigued. That wasn't a straightforward reply, which meant they didn't want him to know, or they didn't like the answer themselves.

'I had a run in with them.' He didn't want to give any details of where or when. His operation with Momentum was supposed to be secret.

A deep voice spoke up. Jake turned to his left to see two pairs of lupine eyes staring at him—the rest of Fallout's body was concealed in the darkness of his alcove.

'Forge are a fledgling organization that are proving to be a thorn in our side. And I for one am glad Hunter has brought this issue up. For too long have the Council sat in silence. Is it because they fear this threat?'

Jake was surprised by the murmurs that circled the chamber. He noticed Amy didn't look pleased that he had raised the issue. Normally he hated these discussions, but now his interest was piqued.

'We are the Council of *Evil*,' snapped Necros. 'We do not fear! They should be afraid of us!'

Fallout laughed. 'But they are not, are they? Instead they taunt us constantly.'

Sidekick

'Is somebody going to answer the question?' asked Jake.

Fallout looked back at Jake. He felt strangely unnerved when all four eyes blinked in a sequence designed to keep two eyes on his prey at all times.

'Forge is a mismatched bunch of rogue Downloaders who have deserted Villain.net and Hero.com. The rumour is that there are even some Primes now joining their organization.'

'If they're both villains and heroes . . . who are they fighting for? And who is leading them?'

'They fight for themselves. They are against everybody and accuse each side of messing up the world. And as to who is organizing them, that remains a mystery.'

'If they're Downloaders, where are they getting their powers from?'

'There have been hacking attacks on both our servers and those of the Foundation,' Necros answered. 'They are technologically gifted, if disorderly.'

'I have heard they have kidnapped Primes and hold them prisoner to extract their powers,' stated Mobius with as much disgust as he could muster. 'We must do something about this menace!'

'Well volunteered, Mobius,' said Necros.

Professor Mobius gave a long hiss. 'I have no time. If Hunter fought them it should be his jurisdiction. He brought the matter up.'

'So be it. Hunter, by Council approval, you are to locate and stop this Forge group.'

Jake considered refusing, but that would make him look overly rebellious. Instead he'd simply accept and do nothing about it. If there was a group of idiots out there trying to play heroes and villains that was some-body else's problem. Not his.

'I'll do it,' he replied.

'Then this meeting is adjourned,' stated Necros.

The end of the meeting meant the chamber doors unlocked—nine separate portals orbiting the room. Eight led directly to the Council members' own private islands. The other led deeper into the main island where the rest of the Council staff lived and all the main work was done.

Jake had been waiting for this moment. The door that led to the island was located in between Momen-tum and Amy's alcoves. The moment the dull thud of hydraulic locks echoed around the chamber, the doors opened—

An ambassador who was about to walk through was decked by a lightning blast as a team of commandos stormed the Council chamber. They showed no mercy in attacking villain and staff alike.

Heads turned in confusion as lightning burst from the weapons the ten commandos carried. They had been part of the shipment Jake and Momentum had stolen in Italy. The commandos' eyes were covered by dark shades that allowed them to see perfectly well in the dim chamber and conveniently concealed their all-black eyes that were a telltale sign that they were being possessed by Momentum.

More ambassadors were hit in the confusion. The Council members didn't have a clue what was happening—the Chamber had never been attacked before.

Jake saw Armageddon was preparing to attack. Jake intercepted and hurtled a super-bright fireball towards the commandos, deliberately aiming wide. The sudden glare from the fireball caused Armageddon to shield his eyes and forced others to look away.

At the same time Momentum ran across the chamber, building his mass and speed with every step. He cut across Necros's line of fire, distracting the super-villain from shooting the commandos. For effect, Momentum cannoned into one of the men, slamming him into a support post of Abyssal's alcove. Stonework cracked under the impact and fell on top of Abyssal's seat. The watery supervillain vanished through a hole in the bottom of his seat like water down a plug. The stones smashed into the empty bath.

While this was happening, the commandos formed a semi-circle around Amy and opened fire. Nine sets of lightning would have torn apart the strongest of people, but somehow Amy survived. She was hurled against the back of her throne, her skin blistered and clothes blackened.

Amy suddenly held out her hands and chanted something in a deep voice. A dark whirlwind immediately formed around her. Jake watched as shadows peeled from the walls to join the tornado. Across the chamber everybody was knocked over by the sudden change in air pressure.

Amy was lifted up by the storm. Leathery tentacles snapped from the whirlwind: they looked squid-like but were barbed with stingers.

The barbs impaled two commandos while another was plucked off his feet by the tentacle and pulled into the maelstrom. Jake was impressed; he'd never seen Amy use her powers before. Momentum had told him about her ability to open up rifts into parallel worlds, worlds where strange creatures lurked to do her bidding. Now he could see how powerful she really was. Jake tossed a couple of fireballs, making sure they fell wide and didn't actually stop the commandos.

Six commandos remained, and they were having difficulty standing. A roving tentacle wrapped around the neck of one and gruesomely decapitated him. Even Jake looked away; it was too gory to watch.

The team was down to half-strength, and Jake

suddenly felt worried their plan to take Amy out would fail.

The other members of the Council all rushed for safety, more concerned with saving their own necks than helping a colleague. Fallout risked a shot—a radioactive pulse that microwaved one of the commandos on the spot.

One commando fumbled for a grenade on his belt. He ducked a slashing appendage and thumbed a button on the grenade. A high-pitched buzz echoed through the chamber, forcing everybody to clamp their hands over their ears.

Momentum's team of scientists had secretly developed the high-pitched frequencies. They interfered with Amy's ability to manipulate dimensions. The frequency raised an octave—and the whirlwind suddenly vanished, taking the tentacled monstrosities with it.

Amy dropped to the ground. She looked astonished that her powers had vanished. The remaining commandos raised their guns at the little girl.

'No!' she screamed.

In three seconds, Amy was dead. So too were the commandos—ripped limb from limb by a combined assault from Mobius, Necros, and Armageddon. There was barely a shred of clothing left. Conveniently all the evidence that could point towards a conspiracy by Momentum and Jake had been vaporized.

Jake tried to act as shocked as everybody else. But inside he could only gloat.

One Council member down, six to go. His surge to power had begun.

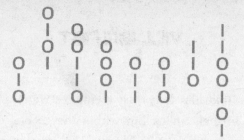

The Hunting Party

In the past, life had consisted of getting into trouble at school or hanging around outside Patel's corner shop with his mates, causing trouble. Boredom forced them to create their own excitement—which everybody branded as 'trouble'.

Now Jake didn't have any time for himself. There was no doubt he never wanted to return to the bad old days. Now he had money and power beyond imagination. Being a member of the Council made him eligible for his first cash card that appeared to have unlimited funds. He heard one person had bought five F-15 fighters on their card, each of which came with a cool twenty-eight million dollar price tag. Jake had yet to spend much. When he had no money it seemed that he wanted to buy everything he saw. Now he was wealthy, there was nothing that caught his eye.

The only thing he really wanted was his family back. And to achieve that he had to convince Pete to form the power that would restore their memories. Jake had once assumed he could create the power himself, but

Grimm told him that their memories were no longer stored in their brains, but within the genetic code of Psych's powers. Jake had to pick his moment to convince Pete to help him.

Jake imagined that once he had Pete's help it would be an easy step to win back his mum and dad. Restoring his sister's memory would be the real challenge. The thought of Beth made his stomach churn. He was responsible for cutting her hand off and hoped that the Foundation hospital had re-attached it. He couldn't bear the guilt if they hadn't.

The assassination of a member of the Council had sent shockwaves across the organization and the place was now crawling with heavily armed security called the Duradan. They were covered head-to-toe in black ceramic armour that had numerous fins and angular vents that made it appear the soldiers were wearing Stealth Fighters. The suits were connected via Wi-Fi to the Council's intranet where they could download whatever powers were needed to deal with a situation.

Jake thought of them as Enforcers with attitude and brains.

Before the forensic teams had cordoned off Amy's seat, Jake examined the area to make sure there was nothing that could lead the authorities to uncover his coup d'état.

The Hunting Party

He poked through a few scraps of charred clothes.

'Find anything?' Necros asked from across the chamber.

Jake flicked a piece of cloth over and saw a small clear pendant, held by a metal cord. He had no idea what it was and quickly pocketed it before it was impounded as evidence.

'Nothing. They've left no evidence,' Jake replied.

Ambassadors buzzed between the shaken Council members.

'This is unprecedented,' commented one ambassador. 'They must have teleported in, which means somebody told them exactly how to get here!'

'Increase security,' ordered Necros. 'Tighten access to the Chamber and monitor everybody arriving and leaving the islands.'

Professor Mobius's sibilant voice rose above a knot of Council members who were arguing.

'This is the work of Forge, I tell you!'

'Rubbish,' snorted Momentum. 'This was a professionally planned attack. These were not amateurs.'

That led to further arguments. Jake was surprised Momentum was defending Forge. They were a perfect scapegoat. Then the mention of his name caused him to listen more closely.

'Hunter will find them, and you will see I was right,' said Mobius brusquely.

All eyes turned to him. Necros nodded.

'The Professor is right. Hunter will find those maggots and bring Forge to its knees.'

Jake felt a sudden stab of anger. What had been a cushy assignment had now turned into an important mission. The pressure was on him to find the real group. That would take up a lot of his time, which is exactly what he didn't want.

He glanced around the chamber, noticing one Council member was missing. He seized the opportunity for more mischief.

'What about Abyssal? He's not here.' Mumbling rose in the chamber as the others noticed his absence. 'He got out the moment the first shots were fired. Never mind Forge, I think you should be looking for him.'

That sparked yet another argument. A few of the Council vouched for Abyssal, but the consensus was against him.

Jake didn't join in. He was feeling tired and weak. He had to get back to his quarters to link up to Villain.net so he could absorb some powers or he would fall unconscious and eventually die. It was the price he paid for being able to absorb powers and create new ones. It was a painful bump in his packed schedule—he still had to track down and meet Pete, and sort things out with Lorna . . . Lorna! He had forgotten about her! It must have been twelve hours or more since he last saw her. He hoped she hadn't snooped around the castle, there were too many clues there that could reveal his real day-job.

As usual, Jake felt his life was slowly spinning out of control. Why could he never get a grip on it?

With a depressed sigh, Pete looked at his reflection in the mirror that hung on the wall of Jake's private Council chamber. His skin was cracked and parched, and an unpleasant blue-green colour. He had lost his thick, free glasses, using his own healing power to correct his vision. Aside from looking like a leper, he was feeling good.

He wore a black jumpsuit that had chunks of ceramic armour protecting his vital areas. The entire suit stretched when his body grew bigger—which was a problem as one of his powers absorbed any impact and transferred the energy into temporarily increasing his size. Jake had given him the suit as a gift.

'Not bad,' said Pete.

'Suits your image,' said Jake. 'It makes you look mean. It's the kind of thing that makes people cower in fear.'

Pete stared at him, checking for any signs of sarcasm. There was none. Pete still didn't trust Jake even though he had revealed to him the dangers of working with

Lord Eon, the first person to offer Pete a mission since he had escaped from the hospital.

Only a few hours ago, Jake had spent some time on Pete's private paradise island that Eon had recently given him for his services. With such an amazing gift, it had been difficult for Jake to convince him that helping Lord Eon would spell the end of the world.

Jake couldn't care less if Pete worked with Eon or not, but he needed Pete alive and his affiliations with the deadly villain put him into unnecessary danger and distracted him from helping Jake.

Jake had been forced to take Pete out and show him some of the horrific destruction Eon had caused. It was enough to convince Pete not to do any further work for the villain—he was feeling villainous, but Pete did have some ethics and destroying the world was not part of his ambitions.

Pete had made his intentions to join Villain.net clear, so Jake had taken him to see Momentum. Jake knew this was technically the second superhero he had brought to the secret island in the last twenty-four hours, but it was necessary. He had to win Pete's trust and show him what the rewards could be.

Jake had put up with Pete's excessive excitement when he had first seen the sprawling island complex. Pete had repeatedly commented on how much better it was than the Foundation's offices. Jake had shown him

The Hunting Party

the V-net system and played security footage of the attack on Amy. Jake was a smooth talker when he wanted something, and he assured Pete that the new space in the Council, opened by Amy's death, would be his.

Pete had become even more excited about this, and his enthusiasm was grating Jake's nerves. However, Jake kept a smile fixed on his face as Momentum had asked Pete to prove his loyalty by offering him a job to collect some rare artefacts from around the world. Jake wasn't really listening, he knew it was linked to Lord Eon, a villain so powerful that both sides lived in fear of him. Jake had his own problems and didn't have time to worry about the rest of the world. Last time he checked it was still there.

Pete accepted the mission and it was left to Jake to offer the ex-hero his new suit.

'Getting the hang of your powers yet?' asked Jake as innocently as he could.

'Slowly. Sometimes they're much too powerful. When I want a warning shot it comes out like a volcano. And I'm not used to absorbing energy. The moment I do my body grows and I lose my flying ability. Why can't I have both?'

'You should work on it. The powers in your body are under your control, even if it sometimes doesn't feel like it. Use them to do what you want.'

'How?'

'Think about calling up one of the powers you absorbed. Keep doing that until you can summon any specific one inside you.'

'What like?'

This was exactly the question Jake was hoping for. 'I've got a friend who got hit on the head and lost his memory. How about trying to summon up something that would cure that? It would really help me out and according to Momentum you have absorbed that power.'

Pete looked at him sceptically. 'That doesn't sound very exciting.'

'But it's a real test. Rather than something as simple as a fireball or lightning bolt, it's a complicated power. Once you master that then less complex ones should come easy.'

'OK. Let's try.'

Pete had grunted and strained but nothing manifested.

'Concentrate harder,' instructed Jake, repeating what Mr Grimm had told him. 'Try to visualize the power.'

A charge of static electricity erupted from Pete's body, shattering the lights, plunging the room into darkness.

'I think that's enough for today,' said Pete drily.

Jake tried to think of an excuse to encourage him

again. Once Pete created the power then Jake had no more use for him. He needed Pete to try harder, but deep down he knew it was pointless. Pete simply wasn't in full control of his powers yet. At least he had volunteered to try and generate the power. That was progress.

They left the room and walked down the brightly lit corridor. Jake's phone buzzed with an email from Momentum: he wanted to see Pete.

Momentum had ended the secure message by stating that the trouble with Lord Eon was eating up too much of his time. Jake would have to continue their plan to destroy the Council of Evil alone for now.

Jake deleted the message. He sensed Momentum was getting cold feet and was using the crisis as an excuse not to go after the other Council members.

Jake dropped Pete off, acting like his new best friend. He could see that Pete still didn't trust him. That was a barrier he'd have to work harder at breaking down.

Jake glanced at his watch—he had to get back to Lorna. Before that, he would make a quick detour to the Research and Development labs to pick up his custom-built ride.

Maybe that would impress Lorna enough so she wouldn't complain that he'd dumped her alone for so long? He hoped so. He also hoped she hadn't wandered

around the castle. He didn't need her asking awkward questions, otherwise Mr Grimm really would insist on 'disposing' of her.

Lorna woke up with a start. A subtle beep had got her attention. She looked around the bedroom and saw a screen had popped out of the top of the bedside cabinet. A flashing message read: DINNER IS SERVED.

Lorna's stomach rumbled as she crossed the room. A quick glance at her phone revealed that she had been in the castle for eighteen hours. It was starting to feel creepy, but at least she had slept through most of it.

She had waited with Chameleon for a while, checking every five minutes to see if her phone had a signal. With nothing to do, she soon felt tired and decided to head back to the warm, comfortable bed.

She yelped when she opened the door and saw that Igor was patiently waiting for her across the corridor. She followed him through a different route than she had explored, down a massive elegant stairway that led to a short corridor and into a large dining room.

Jake sat across the table looking fresh and happy.

'Hungry?'

Lorna took a seat opposite. She felt glum after being dumped for so long. She had wanted to call home to assure her parents she was fine, although she knew the Foundation would have already provided a cover story.

'Where have you been?' She tried not to sound reproachful but failed.

'On a mission. Sorry, things got out of . . . hand.' Jake winced as he was suddenly reminded of his sister.

'Is there a phone around here I can use? I can't get a signal on my mobile.'

'No, sorry. We're in the middle of nowhere.'

'I'm worried about things back home. Is there any word about Emily or Pete?'

Jake drummed his fingers before replying; it was difficult to remember which lies she had been fed. 'The Foundation are still searching for Emily . . . but I don't know any details so don't ask. And Pete . . . he's still missing.'

Lorna opened her mouth to ask about Chameleon but the doors clattered open and Igor rolled in a trolley and set a pair of covered silver platters in front of them. The thought of eating immediately lifted Lorna's spirits and distracted her from her questions. Igor pulled the covers off with all the flair of a waiter in a five-star restaurant. Underneath was a super-sized meal from a burger chain.

'I was expecting . . . something else.' The mouth-watering scent hit Lorna and she could no longer resist the burger. She took a huge bite. Jake smiled and started to eat.

'I was going for pizza but . . . something put me off.' Jake felt sick as he recalled watching Pete eat a pizza earlier, while chunks of his skin dropped onto the food.

'I take it back. This is perfect!' she said between mouthfuls. 'It almost makes up for you leaving me here. Wherever here is.'

Jake sidestepped the probing question. 'My bad, I know. I really need your help. I've got something I can't do alone . . . and I've heard you're fantastic out on missions.'

'Help you out? Do you want me to be your side-kick?'

'Funny. No. I already have one of them.'

'Really? Who?'

Jake hesitated. 'Have you ever heard of a superhero called Blizzard?'

Lorna thought hard. Toby and Pete had spent a considerable amount of time reading the history of the Foundation and all the members who had been and gone. It was a long list, but she was certain she'd heard the name.

'Isn't he dead or retired or something?'

'He's been away from the action for a while.'

'So what's the mission?'

The Hunting Party

Jake had his cover story worked out. 'I've had a report that a notorious supervillain is hiding out in London. We need to bring him down.'

Mr Grimm had been hard at work locating Mobius. The villain had fled there after stating that he no longer felt safe in the Council headquarters.

That had been part of the plan, to instil such fear into the individual Council members that they would leave the safety of the Council hideout and go to their own private sanctuaries where they thought they'd be safe from attack. What they didn't know was that Jake had a list of these super-secret locations and a plan to get into each of them. And the mind-reading Mobius was next on his list.

Jake had decided that bringing Lorna and Munir with him on this attack was a perfect distraction. If anything went wrong the finger would be pointed at the Foundation.

Jake had felt strangely at ease using Lorna as a scape-goat. They got on great and he really liked her . . . even if she was a superhero.

'So this is the ultra-secret mission you got selected for?'

'Yeah. Are you in or out?'

'Count me in.'

She smiled and they 'clinked' their recycled drink cups to seal the deal.

* * *

They could approach London a variety of ways, although Mr Grimm warned that if they teleported or tunnelled in then their arrival would be detected by the Hero Foundation's sensors and Enforcers would be dispatched. London was a national seat of Government and security was ultra-tight. It was a wonder that Professor Mobius had managed to sneak under the radar and establish his secret lair in the heart of the city. Jake thought about that strategy—it was very good if you could get away with it. Hide in the one place the enemy wouldn't think of looking.

Jake had decided that they should fly to the suburbs then take the tube the rest of the way. Jake took Lorna to the hangar to reveal their method of transport.

The hangar was situated in the bowels of the castle and a large portion of it was taken up with a wrecked aeroplane. Lorna peered closely at the aircraft.

'It's a long story,' said Jake fending off her questions. At least he had remembered to use his laser vision to burn off the Airforce One insignia. Now it looked like any other plane.

Jake escorted her to a car-sized vehicle covered by a tarpaulin.

'Check out my new ride!'

The Hunting Party

He yanked the sheet off—revealing a sleek motor-bike. It was the size of a family car with two seats, one behind the other, which positioned the riders so they were leaning forwards. The wheels were huge orbs that pivoted in any direction giving the bike maximum manoeuvrability. It was packed with weaponry and it could fly at speeds approaching mach two. Inspired by Basilisk's SkyKar, Jake had spent a small fortune so the Council boffins could create his SkyByke.

Lorna was impressed. 'Wow! That's incredible! How come you get all these cool gadgets? We never got anything this good.'

Jake tried to act modest, but he wasn't good at it. 'Climb on.'

Lorna sat on the enclosed pillion. It was spacious and comfortable. Jake sat behind the handlebars and gunned the engine. It purred like a lion. He revved the throttle so the engine bellowed across the hangar. He loved this thing!

'Ready? Here we go!'

He had only ridden the SkyByke once when he took ownership and was unsure what all the controls were for. He finally pressed the thumb toggle and a curved transparent energy screen formed overhead to keep the occupants safe. Jake loved the idea of a bike, but he didn't want to get cold and wet riding it.

The hangar doors rolled open, revealing an over-grown runway. Jake accelerated. The bike shot forwards then lifted into the air. Jake roared with delight as they soared upwards like a rocket.

The weather had been terrible the entire flight, but Jake had to admire the machine's instinctive controls. They didn't feel any turbulence at all. The ride was over all too soon as Jake landed the SkyByke in the sub-urbs, making a smooth vertical landing in a narrow street. Jake and Lorna dismounted and he activated the 'baffler'. The Council had started to follow the Foun-dation's lead by implanting superpowers into the elec-tronics. That's what enabled the SkyByke to fly. It also formed an invisible 'baffler' screen around the machine that made people simply ignore the vehicle. Lorna had seen Mr Grimm use a similar power the first time they had met.

He watched Lorna download powers from her mobile phone now that it had a signal. It was the first time Jake had seen Hero.com and he couldn't stop peering over her shoulder. Once she was ready, they continued into the city by tube.

Leaving the warm underground station, they were immediately pummelled by heavy rain. Despite the foul weather the streets were busy. Jake and Lorna pushed their way through a sea of umbrellas, down Charing Cross towards Nelson's Column.

The Hunting Party

Munir was waiting at the base of the column, sheltering under a broad umbrella. It was the first time Jake had seen him since his powers had been restored. Mr Grimm was unsure just how successful the process had been, but Munir looked fit and well. Jake hoped that he would remember they were masquerading as heroes for Lorna's sake.

'Hello, Jake,' said Munir with a smile. Then he turned to Lorna and gave a slight bow. 'And Lorna. I have heard a lot about you from the Foundation. They speak highly of you.'

Lorna was flattered. A scowl flickered across Jake's face. Lorna had been much more fun when he didn't know she was a superhero.

'Are you both ready for this?' Jake asked impatiently. 'We can't afford to mess things up.'

That was an understatement. Overthrowing Amy had been easy enough because she hadn't been expecting it and security was surprisingly lax on the island. Now, every member of the Council was on edge. If Mobius got away then there was the possibility that he'd recognize Jake and the coup would be over.

'I'm ready,' stated Munir. 'More than I have ever been.' He smiled and with the faintest of gestures the rain around them suddenly started to fall as snow. His powers had truly been restored.

They made their way back to Charing Cross station and headed for the underground. It was busy as usual, but nobody paid them any heed. Jake followed the tunnels, looking for a specific door. It looked like any other private door in the tube network. Security cameras monitored the tunnel, but Mr Grimm had already ensured that a loop of the previous hour's commuters was playing. Anybody watching the security monitors wouldn't see the trio enter.

Jake used a telekinetic power to open the lock, exactly as he had done during his escape from Diablo Island. They closed the door behind them, and as usual, nobody gave them a second glance.

Jake looked around the new tunnel. It was circular like the others in the underground and angled sharply down, lit by well-spaced lights held behind cages.

The London underground was the oldest in the world, dating back to the 1860s. Amongst the 250 miles of track there are numerous deserted tunnels, and entire railway stations, that have been closed for both practical and secret reasons. It was to one such area Jake's hunting party was heading.

Lorna pointed to a security camera hidden amongst the bunched cables running around the roof. Jake assured her that Mr Grimm had deactivated them. If he hadn't done so there was no chance they could have got this far without being attacked.

The Hunting Party

They reached a crossroads; the tunnel gently sloped in every direction.

'Which way?' Lorna asked.

Jake stared down each passageway. The silence was deep. He activated an enhanced hearing power and detected the faint sounds of construction. He disabled the power before anybody spoke and deafened him. He pointed to the right-hand tunnel.

'This way.'

'We are heading towards the river. And at this depth . . . under it,' said Munir.

'That's right,' Jake replied. 'There is a storage area under the Thames. That's where we're heading.'

They took the tunnel, and again descended without encountering another soul.

'I'm getting worried,' said Munir. 'Even with the cameras out of operation, we should have triggered some alarms. They may not be expecting us but I would have thought they would be on guard after what happened—'

Jake silenced him with a look. He'd almost blurted about the Council.

'What happened?' asked Lorna.

'We attacked a Forge group in Venice. They know we're after them,' said Jake. He knew he should lace every lie with the truth. It was more believable and harder for him to forget.

'So Munir is right. Why aren't they trying to stop us?'

'Because this is the emergency exit route which they had only opened up a few weeks ago.' Jake smiled. Mr Grimm had obtained the information from Mobius's own database by hacking in through Ernie. Mr Grimm was good, even Ernie had no idea he was being hacked. 'They would be expecting an attack at their front door. There is a monitor along this corridor that detects the use of superpowers. If we use any then the alarm will sound. So we keep walking.'

The entire plan was risky, and Jake was glad he had Munir handy as cannon fodder if things went wrong. He was still struggling to decide if he would help Lorna if she got into trouble, or would he just save his own skin?

Minutes later they saw a metal blast door blocking the path ahead. Jake studied it for a moment. There was no apparent opening mechanism on this side.

'How are we going to get through that?' asked Lorna.

Jake had hoped to find an access panel or a crack so they could slip quietly through. So far he'd been as stealthy as possible, but now it was time to do what he did best.

'With a little brute force!'

He touched the centre of the door and his hand

The Hunting Party

glowed bright green. Radioactive streamers danced from his fingers and the metal melted under his touch. No sooner had he triggered the power than a klaxon began to sound.

'I thought you said no powers?' said Lorna urgently.

'We had to use them at some point. You guys ready? This is going to get wild!'

The entire door glowed then suddenly splashed to the floor as liquid metal—revealing the cavernous chamber beyond.

And sixty guns immediately opened fire on them.

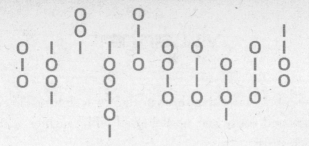

Shelf Life

Jake and Munir swiftly darted aside but Lorna was slower to react. The tennis ball-sized glob of super-hot chemical gunk that shot from the guns took a chunk from her thigh. The heat immediately cauterized the wound as she fell with a scream.

Forty chrome robot troopers were waiting for them, twenty more fired as they ran across the huge cavern to join them. They looked approximately human in shape but were completely featureless. Their bodies were a patchwork of vents and rivets. They reminded Jake of store mannequins. Stubby cannons were bolted onto their wrists and rapidly fired at the moving targets. Behind them, technicians downed tools and fled for the emergency exits.

Jake spiralled overhead, making him a difficult target. Munir bounced athletically from wall-to-ceiling then dropped down amongst the robots. A blast of super-cold radiated from his hands, freezing six of the machines as though they had been dipped into dry ice. Vapour rose from their bodies and Munir finished off the job by punching through the ice sculptures. They shattered easily and he bellowed with laughter with each strike.

'Oh yeah!! Blizzard is back!'

Lorna couldn't stand and was forced to scramble away. Her leg wound was healing—but not fast enough. Four of the robots separated from the herd and took aim at her.

Lorna screamed. It was a sonic wave that made her teeth jangle. The air shimmered and the machines exploded in a mass of limbs.

Jake unleashed radioactive hellfire beneath him. Dozens of robots splintered apart. One ran in circles with no arms, attempting to butt Munir—who froze its head before punching it off. Two others were nothing more than legs running without bodies. It had been a while since Jake had fought with such enthusiasm. It helped that his victims were no match for him. Jake landed on a girder that supported the ceiling. He took stock of the battleground.

Munir turned a section of floor into black ice, causing several robots to slip over. Their flailing cannons helping to destroy more of their colleagues.

Lorna leapt into the air as a dozen robots shot simultaneously. The stone floor bubbled as the chemicals ate through the concrete. She hovered over them and her sonic scream dispatched another wave of attackers.

Shelf Life

Jake thought the operation was going better than he'd expected. Momentum had warned him about overwhelming odds, but they had clearly overestimated Professor Mobius. Beyond the dwindling lines of robots, technicians were scrambling for the exits. Like any other evil operation, they were all hired help who saw their boss's maniacal plans as just another job. They all had friends and family to get home to and Jake felt bad if he had to hurt any of them.

He was about to swoop down on the last of the robots when he did a double take. There was someone walking against the tide of fleeing technicians. It looked similar to the robots, except twice as big and made of a shiny green alloy. Instead of a head, it had a tinted black dome. Behind the dome was what looked like a satellite dish mounted on a gimbal.

Jake had no sooner noticed it than the dish swung in his direction and he heard Mobius's sibilant voice echo across the chamber.

'Traitor! Hunter, you traitor!'

Jake realized that Mobius must be inside the battle armour. The air shimmered like heat haze between the dome and the dish. The dish amplified the signal and a heat ray discharged, knocking Jake off his perch high in the rafters.

Jake hadn't been expecting the ferocity of the attack. His jacket caught fire and he thumped straight onto the ground. He had tried to fly, but for some reason his mind felt foggy.

Icicles shot from Munir's fingers—impaling the last of the robots through the head, destroying their processors. Munir laid an ice track in front of him and speed skated across the cavern to Jake's side.

'Hunter! You're on fire!'

Jake looked at him in confusion, and then he stared at his blazing jacket. Realization was slow to dawn. Munir touched the jacket and frost extinguished the flames.

'Jake, what's the matter?'

'I feel . . . ' He couldn't get the words out. All he wanted to do was sleep.

Munir understood. 'Jake, snap out of it! Mobius is a telepath. He's trying to confuse you.'

Lorna landed next to them.

'What's going ooooonnn—' The last was said as she slipped on black ice and landed hard on her back. Munir was torn between helping her and Jake.

'You will die, Hunter!' screamed Mobius's electronically enhanced voice. 'Your head will be put on a spike for all to see how we deal with your kind.'

'Put a sock in it!' yelled Munir.

Mobius fired again, the shot blasting a support stanchion next to Munir. The older man leapt aside. He couldn't fly, but he had the edge with his agility.

'What is your tag?' scoffed Mobius. 'The Snowman?'

Munir skated in a broad circle, drawing Mobius's attention away from Jake and Lorna.

'I am Blizzard!' he yelled. The thought that attacking a member of the Council of Evil was dangerous did not even cross his mind. In the past it would have taken a legion of heroes to attempt such a feat, but Munir found his new powers intoxicating. He felt more powerful and alive than he had ever done at the apex of his career. Munir raised his ice path off the ground and formed a tight ascending spiral so he could rise above the villain. He fired a volley of razor sharp icicles—

The attack bounced off Mobius's power armour, doing little damage.

'Is that all you can do?' scoffed Mobius. 'You're little more than a fridge on legs.'

The dish tracked Munir's movements. Once again there was a shimmer between the dome and the dish before the heat ray shot out and shattered Munir's ice track. Thirty feet in the air, Munir found himself suddenly falling. He cursed his impetuous attack. Mobius was obviously transmitting his psychic commands from inside the dome and the dish was concentrating and amplifying the power to a far greater degree than Mobius was normally capable of achieving. That knowledge didn't help him as he struck the ground.

Lorna was confused as to why Mobius was calling Jake a traitor. Her thoughts were suddenly derailed as water dripped onto her face. It was coming from a crack in the ceiling where the villain's heat ray had struck Jake. She tried to stand, but Munir's black ice was proving too efficient. She had to concentrate to launch herself into the air.

Jake had wandered away, staggering like a drunk. Lorna noticed Munir was down and looking groggy. The power suit was keeping its distance. Long-range attacks appeared to be Mobius's forte.

She flew over to Jake and grabbed his shoulders. He looked as if he was sleepwalking. She shook him roughly.

'Jake! Pull yourself together!'

Jake peered at her, trying to organize his thoughts. He felt hyper-tired. He feebly shoved Lorna aside.

'Let me sleep.'

Lorna had to admit it was a great weapon, to make your enemy roll over and sleep. Then you could do anything to them.

'If you sleep you will die! Do you understand?'

It looked as if Jake was grappling with the idea. Lorna noticed the power suit was turning towards them. The amplification dish swung in their direction. She pushed Jake aside and launched herself towards the villain, screaming all the way.

Shelf Life

Her sonic waves chewed up the concrete floor, forming a trench that cut straight towards the villain. He didn't flinch—even when the blast struck him with its full force. Machinery behind the power suit exploded but the sound waves had no effect on the green armour.

Mobius chuckled. 'You'll have to do better than scream at me, girl! This suit is made from tyrillium compound! It's the toughest metal in the known universe!'

Lorna had been anticipating some form of victory from a direct attack—instead she now found herself too close to the villain and in his line of fire. An amplified beam shot out—this one formed concentric circles. It was like being pounded by smoke rings.

Lorna banked aside. She felt unharmed.

'Now kill him. Kill Hunter!'

Lorna suddenly u-turned and dived straight at Jake. She couldn't stop herself from accelerating to her top speed. A second later she smashed into Jake so hard that she broke both her arms and Jake was catapulted across the vast cavern, crunching through the glass wall of a set of design rooms that ran along the periphery of the cavern.

Lorna dropped to her feet and stared at her arms, which hung unnaturally limp. She could hear her bones healing, making a sound like popcorn cooking. Tears ran down her cheeks—had she killed Jake?

Jake stood up. He was covered in lacerations from breaking the window, but they rapidly healed. The impact was exactly what he needed to clear the fuzziness inside his head. He stepped from the ruined remains of the office and saw Lorna was crying.

'Jake! I don't want to do this!'

'Kill him!' bellowed Mobius with impatience.

Lorna unleashed her sonic scream at Jake. He took to the air and circled around Mobius—outracing Lorna's scream.

'He's using mind control! Fight him, Lorna! Don't let him inside your head!'

Lorna was trying, but her body was refusing to co-operate. She hoped Mobius didn't know what the third power she had downloaded was.

I see inside your mind, hissed Mobius's voice inside her head. Lorna knew she had just unwittingly given away the nature of the power.

Before Mobius could act on the knowledge, Lorna clapped her hands together. The effect was impressive. A super-bright flash lit up the cavern and a concussive blast-wave rippled out with such force that Mobius was toppled over and more rock and water trickled through the crack in the ceiling.

The flash forced Jake to close his eyes, but he could

still see the imprint on his retinas. The shockwave swatted him out of the air and he landed in a scaffolding tower that had been erected around a large machine at the cavern entrance, which was obscured by white sheets. The aluminium pipes clattered down on top of him.

'Finish the traitor off!' commanded Mobius.

'No!' cried Lorna as she flew, against her will, across to Jake.

He was pushing the scaffolding away, which was pinning him down due to sheer mass. Lorna's mouth opened. She tried to fight the action but it was no use.

Jake looked up at his girlfriend, his thoughts conflicted. He would have blasted any other opponent away, but hesitated because it was Lorna.

A barrage of ice suddenly hit Lorna. The artificial avalanche dragged Lorna aside before she could deliver sonic death.

The power armour twisted to locate Munir. Mobius had been having too much fun being the puppet master and had forgotten Blizzard was still alive.

Munir was standing right behind the suit. He touched the tyrillium armour and ice tendrils shot across it, freezing the machine's joints. Munir could hear Mobius's muffled cursing from inside: the cold had also frozen his external speaker.

Munir speed-skated across to Jake and helped pull off the scaffolding pipes.

'Are you OK?' he asked with concern.

'Yeah. Just my ego thumped a bit.' He glanced at Lorna who was freeing herself from the mound of ice. She didn't look as if she was under Mobius's spell any more. The power suit was immobile. 'Let's blow him to bits right now.' His hands glowed bright green.

'You won't break it open.'

Jake smiled. 'Who said anything about breaking it open? He's going to want to come out of there.'

Jake bounded to the power suit, taking care to stand behind it. He grabbed the shoulders and his radioactive power blossomed in a fierce green light show.

Almost immediately, Munir's ice vaporized and Mobius could move again. He turned round, but Jake piggybacked on the armour, keeping tight hold. His radioactive hands didn't melt the durable metal, and his own body was immune to the heat. But inside the suit, Mobius was starting to feel the rapidly increasing temperature.

'Argh! Get off me!' Mobius twisted and bucked, try-ing to dislodge Jake. It was like being in a rodeo.

Lorna stood up and watched as she rubbed her jaw.

'What's he doing?' she asked Munir.

Munir was impressed with Jake's simple plan. 'He's smoking him out, so to speak.'

Shelf Life

The power armour was now glowing from the radioactive bombardment it was receiving. The armour was maintaining its integrity, but Mobius hadn't designed the cooling system to cope with such extremes.

With a loud snap, the suit slid apart like an extravagant origami puzzle. As plates and flaps moved under him, Jake was finally thrown clear.

Mobius leapt from the mega-hot suit and scampered across the cavern as fast as he could.

Lorna and Munir got their first clear look at the archfiend. His skin was pale green and scaly. His head was enormous—his brain had swollen three times larger because of an accident—bald and covered in veins. His eyes were wide like plates and lacked any eyelids; instead yellow mucus seeped from them to keep them moist. His body looked too frail to carry that enormous head and he was hunched over as he ran. A forked tongue poked from the corner of his mouth, betraying the reptile genes that ran through him.

Munir sprang into action—skating towards the fleeing villain. Mobius glanced over his shoulder and gave a startled yelp as Munir gained on him. A series of worm-like veins throbbed across his head as he triggered his psionic powers.

Munir suddenly slid into an invisible wall with such

force that his nose cracked, a tooth dislodged, and he fell hard on his back. The invisible wall had only lasted for a fleeting second, but because Munir had not down-loaded any healing powers, it was enough to put Munir out of action for a while.

Lorna launched her sonic blast—but Mobius waved his hand and her jaw clamped shut, almost biting her tongue off!

Mobius was heading towards the huge machine that had been surrounded by the scaffolding. Jake took to the air and swooped after the villain.

'Not so brave without your power armour, are you?' he mocked.

Mobius climbed a steep ladder as fast as he could. Jake summoned a fireball and hurled it. His aim was perfect—

Mobius swatted his hand as if swiping a fly. The fire-ball suddenly altered course—straight for Lorna. She barely had time to scream as it hit her in the chest. She was flung backwards, unconscious before she hit the floor.

'Lorna!' Jake was distracted enough for Mobius to reach out his hand and mime grabbing Jake in the air.

An invisible power grabbed Jake mid-flight and he was hammered against the floor, over and over. Even with regeneration powers, it was painful.

'You will die here, traitor! And I'll be going after your family next!'

Then Mobius flicked his hand—and Jake was tossed to the far side of the cavern.

Rage flooded his mind, numbing the pain. His vision became red and his powers churned inside him. How dare Mobius mention his parents! He tried to stand but his body was not having any of it. Jake was forced to lie there as his healing powers pulled him back together, his temper rising—new powers popping in his bloodstream.

Lorna's eyes flicked open and she stood with a groan, her head aching. She was definitely having a bad day today. She had complained to her brother, Toby, that she didn't want to go on any more missions without a suitable reward—yet here she was, doing it all again for nothing.

She saw Mobius at the top of the ladder. He dropped down into the machine beyond. She looked around for Munir and Jake. They were both sitting upright and groaning in pain.

'Will you guys get up?' she yelled. 'The little freak is getting away!'

Jake stood up as the last of his bones repositioned. A deep bellow suddenly permeated the cavern. It sounded like a jet engine powering up. Then there was a massive hiss of compressed air and the high-pitched screech of servomotors.

'I don't like the sound of that,' said Munir through his bloodied lip.

More scaffolding and hanging tarpaulin sheets fell away as something big moved at the end of the cavern.

Jake sighed deeply. 'Aw, no way!'

It was another power suit. This one wasn't chrome green, so he took some satisfaction that it wasn't made from indestructible tyrillium. However, this mechanoid was forty metres tall, following the same design principles of the smaller robots that had attacked them. The 'brain pan' of the head was a transparent dome and they could see Mobius inside, strapped into a control seat, surrounded by banks of equipment.

'Great. That's just what we needed.'

They'd all been beaten black-and-blue by the smaller suit. This was in a completely different league.

The colossal robot moved with a grace and speed that seemed impossible for something so big. It raised a mighty arm to the ceiling and the laser cannon on its wrist—which was the size of a bus—erupted.

Jake had completely ignored the dripping water from the ceiling. Professor Mobius had not. The laser blast ripped the ceiling apart—and the River Thames dropped straight in.

* * *

Shelf Life

Pete Kendall sat back in the luxurious chair and watched the video for the third time. There wasn't much to see, but he still found it captivating.

'Do you understand?' Momentum enquired from across the table.

Since Jake had set off to overthrow Professor Mobius, Momentum had been patiently waiting for Pete to return from his latest mission so they could talk in private.

Pete merely acknowledged the question with a nod. He was watching video footage of Jake placing the MP3 player, with its subliminal message, in the hospital room. Then Jake leaned over and whispered to the comatose version of Pete. The footage was silent, but Pete could hear the words ring in his head:

'Emily . . . she's dead, you know? Your pal Toby killed her.'

Pete had woken from his coma with those words buzzing in his head. He had thought he recognized the voice but hadn't been able to place it. He had blamed his ex-best friend, Toby, and the two of them had fought bitterly. Pete still deeply resented Toby, but now he knew Toby had no part in Emily's mysterious disappearance, he only had one question.

'Why?'

'He wanted you to wake in a terrible rage. If you were furious with your friends then you would be

more susceptible to any offer of friendship and a help-ing hand.'

'And you were part of this?' Pete's fists clenched.

Momentum didn't reveal the slightest concern over Pete's aggressive stance.

'To some degree. I engineered your escape. The binary code that woke you from the coma was mine. I wanted you to wake with full mastery of your powers so you could escape with ease. But I had no part in Hunter's psychological trickery. That is something I don't approve of.'

'You got your way. I'm here. Is this about me getting those stupid artefacts for you?'

On behalf of the Council of Evil, Momentum had been employing Pete's skills to retrieve a series of arte-facts to defeat Lord Eon—a mission that had brought him head-to-head with Toby. He had been told retriev-ing the artefacts could save the world, but Pete didn't care about that. The world was always in danger.

Now it seemed Momentum had ulterior motives. Pete wasn't surprised.

'It's not only about the artefacts. I won't kid you, that mission is very important to me and I thank Jake for suggesting that you do it. I have other contin-gencies in place to get those back, but your help should be properly rewarded. So I am rewarding you with the truth.'

Pete had never thought he could trust Jake after all the bullying abuse he had administered. He was evidently correct.

'Let me guess. You're hoping that I get so mad that I kill Jake, and that will be one less member of the Council for you to overthrow?'

Momentum laughed. It was a deep baritone noise that made Pete's ribs shake.

'Overthrowing the Council was Jake's idea and it suits me fine. He hates everybody, good or bad. This is his surge to power. But if he gets caught then I need to distance myself from him. Worse, if he succeeds in getting rid of everybody else then he'll try to kill me. And I'm not dumb enough to be a part of my own downfall. This is all about survival of the smartest and the fittest.' Momentum chose his next words carefully. 'What do you know of your powers?'

'Only what Jake told me. I absorbed a ton of powers when I kicked Basilisk's backside.'

'Which is why you are of so much interest to Jake. In your system, somewhere, are the powers donated by a hero called Psych. They are the only powers that can restore the memories of his family.' Momentum quickly filled Pete in on Jake's past run of ill-fortune concerning his family. He concluded, 'You are the only one who can help him. The moment you manifest that power, Hunter has no more use for you.'

Pete was furious. 'He can go to hell! I'm not being used by him!'

'Did he tell you anything else? Such as the duration of these powers?'

'He said they might wear off.'

'Oh, they will. Jake is addicted to the powers on Villain.net. His DNA is embedded in the website because he shares the same genes as Basilisk who helped create the site.'

Pete couldn't hide his surprise. 'Jake is related to Basilisk?'

Momentum smiled at the hatred burning in Pete's eyes. 'They're genetic twins, so in a twisted way, I guess he is. There's a bit of the boy in Basilisk . . . a lot of Basilisk in the boy. If Jake doesn't get his regular fix of powers then he will die.'

'Good.'

'You have a similar dilemma.'

Pete felt a shiver down his spine. 'I don't get what you mean.'

'The powers you absorbed will slowly deteriorate and as they do, so will you. Look at your skin. It's disgusting.'

Pete self-consciously scratched his dry cyan cheek. A coin-sized piece of flesh fell off. The wound immediately blistered over. He felt like a zombie.

'You are slowly dying. You absorbed the Foundation's

powers, but you also absorbed an infection that was created by Viral just before he died.'

Pete gasped. Viral was one of the quartet of villains he had been fighting to prevent the Hero Foundation from being destroyed. Viral could create any disease simply by thinking about it.

'Viral's swan song is gnawing away inside you. When your powers go so will you. You have a shelf life, Pete. Then it's game over.'

Pete felt sick talking about his own death in such a casual way.

'Does Jake know?'

'I suspect so. Mr Grimm certainly does.'

Pete sat in silence, pondering his own mortality.

Momentum let him stew just long enough. 'Fear not. I have a cure.'

'What is it?'

'Something to purge the infection from your body. Then you will be able to download from the V-net system without side effects.'

'Give it to me now!'

'I will, Pete, calm down. You're not quite at the end of your shelf life and we both need you to keep this array of powers for as long as possible. I want you to agree to make the cure for Jake.'

Pete frowned. 'You want to help him?'

'No. I want you to agree to fix Jake's parents. I want

you to convince him that you are helping. Then I want you to manufacture this.' Momentum hit a key on his computer and turned the screen so Pete could see it. It was a chemical formula that was beyond Pete's understanding . . . yet something inside him seemed to understand. 'Jake will think it's the memory restorer and will give it to his family.'

'Then what?' asked Pete.

Momentum smiled, and Pete suddenly knew what he was being asked.

'It will kill them?'

Momentum nodded. 'Without them, Hunter will not be the threat he currently is. He will be a sad, confused orphan. Once you have synthesized that for me I will administer the cure to Viral's handiwork.'

It was a diabolical plan—utterly evil.

'And of course you will be well compensated,' Momentum continued. 'How would you like an army of your own?'

Pete's eyes gleamed. He had to choose whose life to save: Jake's parents' . . . or his own.

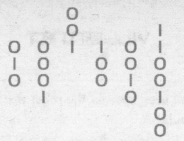

London

A huge whirlpool opened in the Thames as the water was sucked into Professor Mobius's cavern below. A tourist ferry was dragged sideways into the vortex— only by red-lining the engines did the captain avoid being pulled in.

Mobius's huge mechanoid rose from the water, propelled by rockets on its feet. It was awe-inspiring to see the massive robot reach out from the water and grab the span of the iconic Tower Bridge overhead to pull itself from the river. Cars on the bridge swerved aside as huge fingers clawed for purchase.

Beneath the Thames a tidal wave filled the cavern. Jake just had time to grab Lorna before the frothy white water swept them both off their feet. With all the spray he couldn't see Munir, so was forced to leave Blizzard and teleport himself and Lorna to safety.

Prior to the assault, Jake had studied the area around Mobius's base in case he had to teleport out. He had envisioned the riverbank as their destination, and they appeared in a clap of thunder. Nobody paid them any attention; all eyes were on the robot that was hanging from the bridge.

The left foot rocket booster wasn't firing properly and Mobius was having a tough time getting free of the river.

Jake and Lorna took flight and orbited the robot. Jake fired radioactive streamers that looked puny against the giant. They scorched the armour but did little else. It might not be made of tyrillium, but its size made it a fearsome opponent.

'How are we going to stop that thing?' shouted Lorna. She was becoming aware of the crowds forming on both banks of the river. So much for keeping their powers secret—this was a very public display.

A red double-decker bus was trying to speed across the bridge as the robot's other hand clamped around the opposite side of the span. The bus hit a huge finger, and ramped over the hand. Sparks sprayed as it smashed through the road barrier and then it halted, precariously balanced over the edge. The bus was full of terrified passengers who didn't dare move.

'Jake! The bus!'

'I don't care about that! It's Mobius I'm after.'

Lorna shot him a horrified look. 'What kind of hero are you?' Then she shot forward to help the red double decker.

Jake lunged for the robot, and adhered himself to the

London

smooth dome head. Mobius didn't even glance at him. The arch-villain was too busy wrestling with the controls in front of him. Jake shook his hands, replacing the power that charged through them. Now acid dripped from his palms and he pressed against the canopy. The toughened glass began to sizzle as he applied pressure.

Lorna hovered next to the bus. The screaming passengers looked at her in astonishment. She didn't know what to do. The new Hero.com only allowed her to download three powers, and what she had was useless to prevent the bus from falling.

The robot was shifting its weight beneath the bridge, causing the entire structure to wobble. The bus jolted forwards by centimetres. Lorna tried to push it, but it was too heavy. Then a crunching noise got her attention. The road surface was slowly breaking apart. Girders were buckling from the weight of the robot.

Cars had gridlocked the bridge, and now their occupants were fleeing on foot. Some of the bus passengers had the same idea and broke the rear windows, jumping to safety. Those on the top deck were less enthusiastic about leaping out.

A section of glass under Jake suddenly gave way and he fell into the robot's hub, right on top of Mobius. Jake blasted the villain with a blue fireball. Mobius howled, his harness melting under the attack and his right arm taking the full brunt.

The robot lurched and Jake clumsily fell onto the controls, accidentally hitting a series of switches—the entire robot shook as both rocket boosters in the feet ignited.

'What have you done?' screamed Mobius.

Then a lot of bad things happened all at once.

The robot rocketed upwards. The head smashed into the underside of the bridge. The hole Jake had carved in the glass surface had weakened the dome head and it shattered. Both Jake and Mobius had been flattened by the sudden G-force caused by the acceleration. That had saved their lives. The steel girders supporting the bridge slammed down centimetres above their heads.

Lorna could only watch in horror as the centre of the bridge began to rise. Tower Bridge was a bascule bridge, which meant it pivoted open in the centre to allow tall ships to pass through. It was designed to take great weight from above—not a sharp knock from below. The robot blasted upwards, forcing the two halves of the bridge open.

Cars on both sections slid away like toys as the incline became vertical. People still on the bridge suddenly found themselves on a deadly slide as cars plummeted past them.

The initial jolt was enough to nudge the bus over the

edge. Lorna was now flying, pushing against the top deck—but there was no way she could support twelve tons of bus. In fact the weight of the falling bus pinned her down—and they both hit the water at the same time.

As Lorna splashed down, the robot rose out of the water at an angle. Becoming fully airborne, it clipped one of the towers, tearing bricks away. The top section of the tower crumpled from the impact.

The robot cleared the bridge, flames roaring from its feet. Then one of the boosters faltered and the robot spiralled out of control along the river.

The machine rotated onto its back and skipped off the water like a stone. It soared over another road bridge before arcing down two hundred metres later onto a railway bridge. A commuter train was rolling across and took the full brunt of the machine's impact—but the robot's misfiring boosters spurred it on like a rapidly deflating balloon.

It zigged over to one side of the river—shouldered a building, which crumpled from the impact—before barrel-rolling and zagging to the opposite side where it scraped a deep rut across the front of the Tate Modern Gallery.

Jake didn't have time to think about how things had spiralled out of control. His only thought was staying alive.

He used his super-strength to peel himself from the control panel, as the machine wildly pinballed over Blackfriar's Bridge and bounced off more buildings, then skimmed the water as it followed a sharp curve in the river, kicking up a huge screen of water.

The G-force kept Mobius pinned down. He was physically too frail to move. Jake fired a lightning bolt at his enemy—the electricity glanced past Mobius's over-sized temple and sparked the control panels, short-circuiting the faulty systems.

Mobius might have been physically weaker, but he was mentally superior. As the world spun madly around them, he willed Jake to place his fingers against his own head.

Jake was surprised to see the fingers of one of his hands form a pretend gun and press against his temple. He fired a lightning bolt!

Mobius watched as Jake almost blew his own head off. The boy lost his balance and was hurled out of the spinning robot's command centre—plummeting towards the river below.

Jake stopped his fall centimetres over the brown Thames water. He watched as the mechanoid spiralled out of control towards a one hundred and thirty-five metre tall Ferris wheel—more popularly known as the London Eye.

Collision was imminent.

London

***

Lorna fought her way to the surface, taking care not to ingest any of the brown polluted water. The bus was partially afloat but listing dangerously with passengers still leaping from the windows. She looked up—and instantly regretted it.

The two bascules of the bridge fell back down with such crushing force they ripped free of the towers. The electro-hydraulic rams that held the bridge up snapped and a sixty-one metre section of road fell towards her—

Lorna tried to fly from the water, but suddenly found that her foot was trapped and she fell back into the water . . . or rather onto hard ice.

The entire Thames had frozen, and her foot was held fast. People who had been treading water were now held in the ice, screaming from the biting cold. At least the bus was no longer sinking and the remaining passengers could jump onto the ice.

Thick columns of ice shot from the water to stop the falling bascules. The temporary support columns groaned from the impossible weight, but they held. There was only one person who could have saved her.

'Blizzard!' she said, careful to use the man's alias in public.

Munir was looking around the winter wonderland in

amazement. Then he came to his senses and pulled Lorna from the ice. At his command the ice released her.

'That was amazing!' she said.

Munir was shocked. 'I was never this powerful.'

'What do you mean by that?'

Munir hesitated—then the sound of twisting metal grabbed their attention. It was coming from the London Eye.

Lorna flew the short distance. Munir speed-skated along the river. They both watched the mechanoid become entangled with the London Eye. The Ferris wheel's supporting A-frame snapped under the pressure—and they both toppled sideways onto the corner of an impressive old building behind them: the County Hall.

People fled in panic as the building's wing was demolished. The robot lay in the wreckage, fizzling and sparking.

'Where's Jake?' asked Lorna looking around.

There were too many people running from the scene. Then Munir pointed. Jake dropped from the air, landing on the machine's scorched chest.

The side of Jake's face was blooded, with torn flesh hanging from his jaw. Lorna and Munir joined him. Lorna grimaced in disgust when she saw his face. Even though the flesh was now forming over the wound, the grotesque sight had turned her stomach. She felt a wave of sympathy for Jake.

Heavy wheezing came from the cloud of dust that had rolled over the impact site. Professor Mobius limped from the broken machine's cockpit. He staggered across the robot's chest before he saw his three nemeses.

'You think you have won, Hunter?' The villain's reptilian tongue stroked across his bloodied cheek.

'I know I have, Mobius. You're the second to go,' replied Jake.

'So you arranged Amy's assassination? And you think you can bring them all down.'

'I'm doing a pretty good job.' Jake's face had now completely reformed and he could finally smile. It was cold and ruthless.

'But why? We offered you a place with us. I was one who actively campaigned for you when we discovered Chromosome's treachery. What have I done to you?'

Jake shrugged. 'I had to start somewhere.' It was a callous answer, but he hated each and every one of the Council members equally. 'If it wasn't for you and your kind, Villain.net would not have existed. I would not have gone through hell and back with my family, and I wouldn't be addicted to your stupid powers.'

Jake was focused on his enemy. He didn't see Lorna looking at him with increasing concern.

'It is not us who have twisted your sister as a weapon against you!'

'The other side are just as bad. They're next. There's only going to be one superpower left on this planet—and you're looking at him!'

Lorna glanced at Munir. The swarthy hero was staring straight at Mobius, his face unreadable. She jabbed him in the ribs.

'What's Jake talking about? What aren't you telling me?'

Munir looked at her, then it dawned on him that Lorna was not in on Jake's alter ego as the Dark Hunter.

'All is not what it seems,' he said in a sharp whisper.

Lorna was confused. There were so many conflicting things happening around her that it was difficult to see whose side anybody was really on. She had the distinct impression she was being toyed with.

Jake stepped menacingly towards Mobius.

'Time to die.'

Mobius hissed defiantly. It wasn't quite the reaction Jake had been expecting. At that moment the dust began to clear, borne by a gentle breeze. Jake caught Mobius's subtle jerk of the head. He followed his gaze.

Several hundred people stood motionless around the impact site. Some had debris in their hands, using it as clubs. Jake even saw several armed police. They all looked at Jake with blank expressions typical of mind control.

Mobius chuckled. 'You clearly underestimate the Council leaders. We could not rise to the position we're in if we were so easy to kill.'

Jake noticed Mobius was absently stroking a pendant around his neck. It looked similar to the one he had snagged from the Chamber floor when Amy had died. Did all the Council Members have one? What were they? He forced his attention back to the problem at hand.

'Blizzard, Lorn. Get ready to fight.'

They didn't answer. Jake had a sinking feeling as he turned around.

Munir and Lorna were staring at him with the same blank expressions.

Professor Mobius's incredible mind control powers meant that he had Jake surrounded by a thousand strong mob—and they were all innocent victims.

Leaving the Council of Evil's island was unusually difficult for Mr Grimm. Since the assassins had teleported onto the islands, the Council's unofficial leader, Necros, had declared marshal law and nobody could arrive or leave the island using superpowers. Ernie, the artificially intelligent computer, had activated power dampers that negated all known forms of super-travel and the Council's own Duradan warriors enforced this rule with brutish enthusiasm. The rule didn't apply to the Council members, obviously. There was only one section of the island people could travel from, and that is where Mr Grimm had been forced to queue for twenty minutes before he was allowed to depart.

He arrived at one of the Hero Foundation command centres. Since the destruction of the Foundation's main headquarters, security had been tightened there too, but it still felt liberal compared to the iron fist that was crushing the Council of Evil.

Mr Grimm never gave any of his thoughts or plans away. He was too smart for that. While he had been discussing with Jake about the downfall of the Council of Evil, he had made sure his fingers were in many other pies, including the chief business that was consuming the Foundation. All their heroes were combing the world looking for ways to stop the threat of Lord Eon. Grimm was used to the world's threat levels being high, but this really was the edge of a cataclysm. However, there was no role for him in that particular mission so he tried to shunt it from his mind. He was here to keep his appointment with Eric Kirby on another project that he had been involved with.

Mr Grimm adjusted his tie before entering the room, perfectly on time as usual. Eric Kirby looked through a window at the obstacle course below. He didn't even bother turning round. Mr Grimm joined him.

'How goes the search for the Time Dilator?' Grimm enquired. He hated small talk. To him it felt unnatural and clunky.

'It could be better. Could be worse. We've got our best people on the job. Well, after that incident with Pete . . . ' Kirby trailed off. He had been deeply hurt by the traitorous behaviour of what he could only now refer to as 'the Pete incident'.

'It is a shame,' said Grimm without a modicum of emotion. He knew the truth about 'the Pete incident'. In fact he knew more about that multi-layered problem than anybody else.

'I wonder if we did the right thing setting up Hero.com,' said Kirby sadly. 'Sometimes I think it does more harm than good.'

'Without it, Villain.net would prevail.'

'It's because of it that Villain.net exists!'

'And without either perhaps all Primes would have disappeared in a cloud of mutually assured destruction.'

When Kirby next spoke it was almost a whisper. 'Maybe we should have. We were dying out for a reason.' In the past there had been many primes, many heroes and villains, some who had passed down into legend. Their numbers dwindled as fewer and fewer

Primes were born into society. These days new Primes are very rare indeed. 'Maybe we should be extinct, like the dinosaurs.'

'Dinosaurs were dumb animals who could not fight back the ravages of catastrophe and evolution. We can.' Grimm was eager for a change in the morbid conversation. 'How is our agent?'

'Getting better with each simulation. Burning with the thought of revenge, as it happens.'

They both watched Beth Hunter navigate the automated obstacle course below, firing energy pulses at automatic guns and moving targets. She was fast and lethal.

'Thoughts of revenge will have to burn bright if she stands any chance of beating Dark Hunter,' said Mr Grimm as he watched.

He had helped Kirby develop Jake's sister into the perfect nemesis. Grimm likened Jake to a savage guard dog—great to use to keep people in check, but you always had to have something to beat the dog with should it ever decide to bite your hand.

'Have you had any luck in locating Hunter?'

As usual, Grimm had plans for Beth and Jake, and he wasn't prepared to betray his best soldier to Kirby. He knew where Hunter was at any given time.

'No. He has vanished off the radar. But as soon as he surfaces you will know.'

London

Kirby seemed preoccupied. He was wrestling with telling Grimm a secret. Eventually he caved in. 'I have a mole in Jake's operation,' said Kirby.

Mr Grimm experienced something he very rarely did: a knot in his stomach. If Kirby had somebody spying on Jake then it was only a matter of time before they reported seeing Grimm with him . . . unless it was a hint that Kirby suspected Grimm of being a double agent. Grimm kept his poker face and waited for Kirby to elaborate.

'An agent deep undercover. But I haven't heard anything back from them yet.'

Grimm felt the knot relax. Good—his secret was safe. But it was only a matter of time.

'And who is this agent?'

'I don't want to say too much. It was difficult getting them in position. All I will say is that we have to make sure our undercover agent is not harmed in any attacks we plan from here on. They're too vital an asset.'

'Of course. I completely understand. But with knowing who to look out for . . . '

'You'll know. It will be the one standing with him who isn't a villain.'

Grimm thought of the potential suspects—Lorna, Munir . . . or could it even be Pete? They were, or had been, heroes. Mr Grimm didn't see himself as a traitor even as he played both sides. To him, traitors were weaselly cowards who should be exterminated.

He had to find out which one of them was the mole before his cover was blown.

Unless he could get rid of them all.

Fight or flight. That was Jake's only option.

If he left now, then Professor Mobius would escape and the Council of Evil would know about his plan. If he tried to attack Mobius then he would have to fight a thousand innocent people—including Munir and Lorna—and it was obvious that would lead to some fatalities.

'What's the matter, Hunter? Scared of hurting your little friends? Or does defeat terrify you?'

Jake had to make a hard decision. He had to think about himself.

A shimmering surge of energy suddenly hit Mobius, forcing him to his knees. It radiated out across the crowd without mercy. Like dominoes falling, several hundred people were thrown a dozen metres. Some landed on the frozen river, others were dragged painfully over the ruins of the County Hall wing and remains of the London Eye. Jake didn't see what happened to Lorna and Munir, as it all happened so fast. The fleeting thoughts about Lorna's welfare were

London

brushed aside when he realized that energy surge hadn't come from him!

A figure landed next to Jake with such force that the impact made the robot's hollow chest *bong*. It was Pete. Despite the dry cyan skin that made him look permanently ill, he was the best sight Jake had seen all day.

'Heard you were in town,' grinned Pete. 'Thought you might need a hand.'

Jake was flabbergasted. The victim of his thoughtless bullying had now saved him.

'How did you do that?' was all Jake could manage.

'I'm learning to control my powers. I'm finding out a lot of things,' said Pete.

Jake turned back to Mobius, who was on his back and groaning. He had lost control of his mob. Jake could hear the wail of a hundred injured people. Jake would have attacked them if he had to, but Pete had done it as a favour. What kind of person would do that?

Jake marched over to Mobius and ripped the pendant from his neck.

'What is this thing? Have you all got one?'

Mobius didn't answer. He rolled over and tried to crawl away. Jake planted his boot in the small of the villain's back.

'End of the line, pal,' snarled Jake—then unleashed the final blow.

Two down.

A Helping Hand

Pete circled the SkyByke, eyeing it enviously.

'Where can I get one of these?'

Jake looked at him impatiently. 'Help me with my problem and I'll give it to you.'

Pete tried to avoid his gaze, keeping his attention on the bike. 'Sure.'

If it hadn't been for Pete's unexpected arrival in London, Jake would have been forced to use his powers on the entire crowd of innocent onlookers, or risk being beaten by Mobius. They had teleported back to the SkyByke, and then Jake had taken them back to his castle. Before he left, he'd spotted that Lorna and Munir were still alive. He assured himself that Munir would look after her; he might be a turned hero but that didn't mean he was all bad. Munir had a tracking beacon that would enable him to return directly to the castle with Lorna. Jake felt a wave of guilt at leaving his girlfriend behind. He would have to make up some excuse for abandoning them.

Jake studied Pete again. He was thankful for Pete's arrival, but suspicious.

'How did you know where to find me?'

Pete shrugged, poking the SkyByke to test its sturdiness. 'Mr Grimm mentioned it.'

That sounded perfectly reasonable to Jake. He pulled out the sonic-extractor from his pocket. Fortunately it was still in one piece, even after all the punishment Jake had been through.

'Are you ready to do that favour for me and create that power for my friend that lost their memory?'

'Then what?'

'I can take a sample with this little gizmo and use it on my friend.'

Pete hesitated, then nodded. 'OK. Let's do it.'

Pete's skin was bluer than usual. Jake thought he looked nervous.

'Are you feeling all right?'

'I'm a bit preoccupied. I have to go to Japan soon. A mission for the Council. So let's get on with it. A power to restore your friend's memory?'

'You absorbed Psych's power. It's in you somewhere. You just have to concentrate hard to manifest it.'

Pete was starting to sweat. He nodded and closed his eyes. He thought hard . . . hard about the complex symbols Momentum had shown him. Pete wasn't taking any joy from his actions, but he kept telling himself

A Helping Hand

that Jake had never done him any favours. Jake was equally as responsible as his ex-best friend, Toby, for making his life unbearable.

He convinced himself that Jake deserved everything bad that happened to him.

Yellow sparks flickered in Pete's hand. He held it up and focused. A gentle amber aura caressed his fingers.

Jake was mesmerized. There was the power to fully restore his parents' memories. He could finally get his family back! Administering it to Beth might be tricky, but once he did she would stop attacking him. Things were finally turning his way.

'Hurry and capture it!' snapped Pete.

Jake hurried forward and placed the nozzle of the sonic-extractor against Pete's finger. He squeezed the device's trigger and the tip glowed red. Pete felt a warm tingle flow through his hand and saw the amber glow get sucked into the device. In seconds the extractor stopped and a green light blinked on the hilt.

'Is that it?' Pete asked as he vanquished the power.

Jake gazed reverently at the device. 'I think so.' Then he pulled his gaze away and looked at Pete. For a second Pete thought Jake was going to cry, instead Jake held out his hand.

'Pete . . . I'm sorry for all the stuff I've done to you in the past. I was a real idiot. You're a mate. Anything you want, I'll help you get.'

Pete didn't know what to say. He limply shook Jake's hand and felt the sudden desire to be somewhere else before his treachery was uncovered. Try as he might, he couldn't shake the feeling of dread he got from hanging around Jake. Pete mumbled something then teleported out of the hangar.

Jake looked at the new power in his hand. He didn't have a moment to lose. The SkyByke would only slow him down so he excitedly opened a quantum tunnel and stepped through into his parents' house.

Jake looked around the kitchen. It looked familiar and comforting. He couldn't stop grinning despite the fact he knew Enforcers watched the house, waiting for his arrival.

Jake crept towards the lounge. He could see the back of his mum and dad as they snuggled together watching the news on TV.

He recalled Mr Grimm's instructions. All he had to do was squeeze the trigger and the sonic-extractor would deliver the correct dose into his parents.

Easy.

His mum was the nearest, but he didn't want to startle her. In the past, their minds had been altered so they were unable to see him. He had had some success in reversing the process with the power Psych had

A Helping Hand

given to him before his unfortunate death. Now they were able to see him, but couldn't remember him.

Jake closed his eyes and summoned one of the super-powers buried in his genetic make-up.

He turned invisible.

Confidently he stepped out and in front of his mother. She looked right through him, with a quizzical frown. For a second Jake thought she could sense him, but then he realized that she was only reacting to something she saw on the news, something about a town in Africa vanishing.

Jake carefully leaned forward, getting in position with the nozzle of the extractor hovering over her temple.

She suddenly turned away to look at her husband, ruining Jake's shot.

'Do you want a drink?' she asked.

'Dammit!' swore Jake.

His parents' heads suddenly looked around, their eyes wide with fear. His dad was first off the couch.

'Who the hell said that?'

Jake's blood ran cold—he was invisible, not silent! He backpedalled straight into the TV. The wafer-thin plasma toppled backwards off its stand, the screen cracking from the impact.

'It's a ghost!' screamed his mother. 'Is anyone there?'

Jake rolled his eyes. His window of opportunity was shrinking.

He darted forward and shoved the extractor against his mum's head. He squeezed the trigger.

A yellow haze suddenly enveloped her head. She screamed, her hands swatting it as if it was a swarm of flies.

'Argh! Get it off me!'

Jake watched as his dad reacted—shoving his wife onto the sofa.

'Susan! You're possessed!' he cried and began hitting her head with a pillow.

Jake saw his chance and injected the power into his dad's head. His dad screamed and fell to his knees—but not before lashing out and punching Jake in the face.

Jake toppled into a glass cabinet that mostly displayed Beth's trophies. His invisibility immediately wore off. He clambered to his feet, wiping the glass shards from him.

'Mum! Dad! It's me! It's Jake!'

But they were ignoring him. The energy bloom sank beneath their skin, causing them to scream louder. Jake's optimistic smile wavered as they began clawing their own faces, drawing blood.

'Stop that!' he said, trying to wrest his father's hand away. His dad didn't even look at Jake as he shook him off.

The skin on their faces undulated as if something was

A Helping Hand

trying to escape. They both fell still; their skin looked heavily bruised.

'Mum? Dad?' Jake couldn't bring himself to touch them. 'Say something?' Tears now streamed from his eyes. Something had gone terribly wrong. He willed his arms and legs to function, and knelt down feeling for a pulse. He'd had a first aid lesson at school once, and, as usual, had messed around with his mates rather than listen.

He might have accidentally killed his parents.

The bay window suddenly imploded and a vengeful figure dropped from the sky.

'You've killed them!' screamed Beth Hunter.

Munir ran his hand along the SkyByke.

'Looks like he beat us back here.'

Lorna scowled. She had been worrying about Jake. The final events in London had occurred so quickly that all she remembered was a massive shockwave knocking her, Munir, and hundreds of others onto the frozen river. When they had finally got back to the action, Jake had gone and Professor Mobius was dead.

They had tried to calm the situation, and, with thousands of confused civilians, it wasn't an easy task. When the first chopper load of Enforcers approached, they took the opportunity to leave. Munir didn't think it was wise to hang around and try to explain what had happened.

Now they were back at Jake's base, Lorna had a number of questions buzzing through her head, all of which she was reluctant to share with the older man. She hated the fact that Munir appeared to know more about Jake than she did, and after the confusing experience with Professor Mobius she didn't know who to trust. She wanted to trust Jake, but his actions had been questionable, and when Mobius had called him a traitor . . . There was definitely something Jake was keeping from her, but she couldn't work out what it was.

'I think we should make ourselves at home and await the return of our host,' said Munir. They headed up from the hangar into the body of the castle. There was no sign of either Jake or Igor and all the lower floor doors were locked.

Munir excused himself and left in search of a shower. Lorna had no intention of sitting down and waiting. She wanted answers to some very pressing questions. She decided to start with Chameleon, but found the door was still locked. She didn't possess the skeleton-key power and convinced herself that Jake had probably already returned Chameleon to the Foundation. She continued exploring and found herself at the sealed metal door at the base of the spiral staircase.

A Helping Hand

She thumped on the door. Something of obvious importance was behind it. All the secrets were making Lorna feel angry. She futilely kicked the door.

'Open up!' she shouted, booting the door again and hurting her foot. She screamed in pain and frustration—

Her sonic blast ripped the reinforced door off its hinges. She shut up in surprise as the door clanged against the steps beyond. Using that power hadn't occurred to her. Lorna held her breath, waiting for the sound of approaching footsteps that would have surely been alerted by the noise.

No one appeared. She propped the door to one side so it wasn't immediately obvious to a passer-by, then ran up the steps.

Lorna found herself at the top of a tower in Jake's Command Centre. It was daylight outside, and she was rewarded with a stunning view of sunlight streaming over the jagged snow-capped Carpathian mountains. Brooding clouds clung to the peaks, slowly advancing onto her position.

In the centre of the room was a curved table with several computers and monitors all on standby. Several large plasma screens played world news channels; one was focusing on the events in London.

She sat in one of two luxury leather chairs and took it all in. She nudged one of several computer mice on the table. A screen flicked to life with a digital map of the world, the perfect tool for helping visualize any place in the world if you wanted to teleport there.

She nudged another mouse. The screen flicked to life. It was Hero.com, with a weird red colour scheme. She quickly browsed through the icons, noticing some unfamiliar ones. Lorna was about to move away when the page scrolled to the top. It didn't say Hero.com—it said Villain.net.

Here we go again, thought Jake as his head cracked through the plasterboard of the living room wall. His momentum carried him straight into the brick load-bearing wall. His teeth jangled from the impact and he dropped onto a sideboard that splintered under his weight.

He lay there, not sure what to do. Had he just killed his parents? And now his amnesiac sister was on a murderous rampage.

Jake felt a telekinetic force grip his collar and accelerate him upwards. He smashed through the ceiling and found himself being slung like a rag doll into Beth's room.

Why had they reacted so badly to the power he had administered? He had given them Psych's power before and they hadn't reacted. Why now?

A Helping Hand

He heard Beth's footsteps on the staircase. That was typical of his sister—she had trashed half the house, but still felt it was improper to run up the stairs.

Perhaps he had used the power incorrectly? No, he knew that wasn't right. There was no reason for it not to work.

Unless . . . unless Pete had produced the wrong power.

Mr Grimm had been confident that couldn't happen. The power was within Pete already. All he had to do was call it up. Like Lorna and the rest of her friends, Pete had been downloading powers for the same length of time as Jake, so he was now experienced enough to call up the correct power.

The revelation hit Jake hard: Pete had conjured up the wrong power. He had planned for this to happen!

A seething rage consumed Jake. He recalled the look on Pete's face, and the eagerness with which he had changed his mind. He had been set up! Pete was too naïve to act on his own, somebody must be using him.

Anger coursed through Jake, and he felt his powers flare. Beth chose that moment to enter. The door opened two centimetres before green plasma leapt from his fingers and blew it off its hinges. Beth was hurled backwards.

Jake didn't want to fight. He charged through her bedroom window to fly away—

Anger had clouded his mind. He forgot Beth was negating his transport powers with her snag-net gizmo. He plummeted into the garden, breaking his arm. Jake jumped to his feet, clutched his injured arm to his side and ran.

The street was filling up with inquisitive neighbours who had heard the explosion when Beth struck the house. Several people blocked Jake's path.

'Are you all right, lad?' asked one concerned neighbour who failed to recognize Jake.

Jake snarled and blasted the man in the chest. The crowd collectively screamed as the man crunched into the windscreen of a car. Jake heard somebody shout: 'He's got a gun! Call the police!'

A muscular man, who Jake vaguely recalled owned his own gym, tried to tackle Jake to the ground. Luckily, his broken arm had now healed so he could hold the man at arm's length.

'You don't know who you're messing with!' snarled the man.

Jake shoved the man hard—so hard he flew ten metres in the air before crash-landing in somebody's garden.

'Keep away from me!' growled Jake as his eyes burned red. He was fighting to control his temper. The crowd edged away from Jake as his hands glowed green. He saw no sign of Beth—with any luck she was helping their parents.

A Helping Hand

The thunderous sound of helicopter rotors heralded the arrival of two Chinooks, packed with Enforcers. Jake sprinted away as fast as he could. He needed to get out of the snag-net's zone of influence so he could teleport to safety. He had a plan.

He thumbed a small homing beacon in his pocket. With a loud bang, Jake's SkyByke teleported next to him. Most of the onboard tricks, such as flight, were powered by harnessed raw superpowers so would be redundant around the snag-net. However, the bike still had a powerful 300 horsepower engine.

Jake jumped aboard and flicked the ignition. The bike roared off, echoing down the street like the bellows of hell.

Jake skilfully threaded the motorcycle around parked cars and was soon on a major road. He forced the engine to give everything it had. The rational part of his brain told him to get away from his sister because, if they fought, Jake was in such a foul temper that he would probably kill her.

He checked the rearview monitor, which was linked to a high-definition camera in the SkyByke's tail. Beth wasn't following him, but one of the Enforcer helicopters was.

The twin-rotor craft was metres over the road, the wide blades spanning the entire street, and on occasion, clipping trees. Gunfire erupted from the chain gun mounted under the fuselage. The SkyByke was incredibly nimble, even at full speed. The spherical wheels enabled Jake to jink aside, almost at right angles, from the bullets.

A strange calm gripped Jake. His normal tendency would be to blow the Enforcers from the sky, but after taking out two members of the Council of Evil the good guys seemed like a trivial problem.

He had assumed he'd killed his parents—but the absence of Beth hot on his heels indicated she was still with them. Which meant they must be alive. Jake knew he was grasping for any positive angle, but it was all he had left.

Even his desire to kill Pete had dampened, replaced by icy calm reasoning. He still needed Psych's power that resided inside Pete. And now he needed to know who had used Pete as a pawn, and why? What possible advantage could be gained from making Jake kill his own parents? His money was on Momentum—out of everybody around him, he was the one Jake trusted the least, although he had no proof. He would have to find that.

Bullets chewed up parked cars to Jake's left. He skidded the bike around a sharp corner. The Chinook went wide, the undercarriage taking down a telegraph pole.

Jake needed to lose his pursuers. He red-lined the engine, taking corners as sharply as possible. The

A Helping Hand

Chinook stuck to him like glue. But Jake had the advantage, this was his home turf.

Jake took a blind corner at full speed—the aircraft followed, straight for a tunnel mouth!

The SkyByke shot through the tunnel at 180 miles per hour. He glanced in the mirror and was disappointed to see the Chinook hadn't slammed into the tunnel as he'd planned. The pilot brought the machine to a sharp stop before the collision.

On the other side of the tunnel, Jake's instrument panel lit up. His flight controls were active. He was out of Beth's snag-net radius. He engaged the flight control and the bike soared up.

As the earth spiralled away from him, Jake cleared his mind of the hundred little schemes for power he had been engaged in. He was called Dark Hunter.

It was time to stop messing around and start hunting.

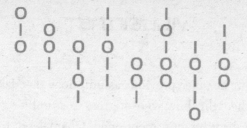

A Traitor Within

Lorna raced down the tower steps; her legs were such a blur she feared she would trip. She ran out into the corridor and stopped to catch her breath.

Why had Jake been looking at Villain.net? There had to be some mistake. They had just defeated a major supervillain in London—it didn't make any sense.

The confusion Lorna had been experiencing was beginning to form into cold fear in the pit of her stomach. She trusted Jake. She had helped him when nobody else would. What was he up to?

While they were waiting for the Enforcers to arrive in London, Munir had confided to Lorna that Professor Mobius was one of the Council of Evil.

If Jake had been targeting the Council then perhaps he was using Villain.net as a conduit to get to them? That made sense, and would explain why Mobius had called him a traitor. She liked the idea of Jake as an undercover agent for the Foundation. After all, Jake had saved Chameleon . . .

Hadn't he? Her previous assumptions that Jake was doing the right thing were starting to crumble.

Why had he not mentioned Chameleon to her? Surely saving one of the Hero Foundation's star heroes was something to brag about? Had he handed Chameleon over yet?

Lorna could kick herself for not bringing it up in conversation. She was starting to feel she'd trusted Jake a little too much.

Anger gripped her. She was nobody's fool. She moved to the staircase, intending to check if the Chameleon statue had been moved. She stopped in her tracks when she heard the sound of glass shattering. It sounded muffled, as if somebody was trying to do it stealthily. It came from the opposite end of the long corridor.

She tiptoed across, although there was no need with the thick carpet. It was coming from the end room. She risked a peek in—and swallowed her scream.

Igor was slumped against the wall. A pair of icicles were embedded in his chest, pinning him to the stone beyond. The projectiles' intense cold had frozen the wounds, so thankfully there was little blood. His face was pale, still in the rictus of pain. Lorna shuddered; Igor was dead. Murdered.

The ice was a dead giveaway to who his attacker was. Munir stood across the room with his back to her. He was chipping away at the wall. Lorna tried to get a clearer view.

Munir had frozen the stone blocks on the wall and was shattering them. Now he was pulling chunks of super-frozen stone away to get at something beyond. Lorna caught a glint of silver.

With a few more strikes, Munir had cleared away a substantial hole. There was another wall beyond the stone made of silver panels. Lorna frowned. From this distance they looked like giant circuit boards.

Then she noticed part of the ceiling had been torn away and the circuit board theme continued up there, although these ones ran diagonally across the ceiling. Lorna quickly deduced that they must run to the centre of the castle.

She ducked away before Munir caught her. She'd seen enough to know he was a murderer. But what had he uncovered behind the wall? She brushed that thought away. He was obviously a villain who had wormed his way into Jake's company. She would have to tell Jake as soon as possible.

However, something still gnawed at her. She quietly crept down the staircase to the room where she had found Chameleon.

Lorna hesitated at the locked door. She could still feel her fading superpowers—the download time was expiring, and with no phone signal, she was unable to download any more. She put her lips to the lock and gave a sonic scream. It was little more than a sonic-croak—but it was enough to crack the internal locking mechanism without leaving any evidence on the outside.

She entered and was surprised to find Chameleon was still there. Lorna ran a hand across the smooth crystal surface. Why was he still here? She looked at her phone and wished she could call the Hero Foundation.

Lorna knew the dangers of shattering the person held inside, but the crystal around Chameleon looked different. She was fairly sure it was a casing and that the hero inside was still flesh and blood. She would try and break a little off.

She focused her sonic-croak, which was now little more than a wheeze. The weak shockwave was substantial enough to crack an area around Chameleon's hand.

She tried again, careful to focus the blast on the hand. The crystal splintered away—fortunately Chameleon's hand didn't. Instead the reptilian claw flexed—then frantically indicated to the rest of him. Lorna got the message.

'Don't worry, I'll get you out.'

She stepped back and increased the level of her scream. She didn't want to alert Munir or harm

A Traitor Within

Chameleon so it took three attempts before Chameleon's prison shattered.

The hero slumped to the floor, weak and dehydrated. His body twitched then snapped from the hunched reptilian form to his regular shape of a handsome young man with jet-black hair styled into a widow's peak.

Lorna cradled his head. 'Don't worry, you're safe now. I'll get you back to the Foundation.'

Mr Grimm watched Jake restlessly pacing his private chamber in the Council of Evil.

'What do you mean, a traitor?'

Mr Grimm took a deep breath. 'You know as much as I. Kirby has somebody on the inside.'

'Munir?'

'How about Lorna? Or Pete?'

'I brought Lorna to the castle. She still thinks I'm a hero. It's not her.'

'And you brought Blizzard and Pete to this island! If the Council learn that you have brought any of those heroes here, they will punish you. Like they punished Chromosome.'

Jake shivered at that thought. He had watched Chromosome get disintegrated before his very eyes by the Council members. That was when he had been offered the position.

'If I really had a traitor in my ranks, then why haven't they done anything yet? I have brought two of them here, why wait?'

Mr Grimm became pensive.

'You have also taken them to the castle. They're there now.'

'So?'

A rare flash of anger crossed Grimm's face. He thumped his fist on the table next to him. 'That was your place of solitude! Somewhere nobody could find you!' He took a deep breath and calmed. 'It's . . . a special place.'

Jake remained silent. How could he be so stupid? He had allowed his enemies access to all his secrets. He refused to believe it was Lorna. Pete was an obvious choice—but he was also an enemy of the Foundation so Jake doubted it was him.

Which left Blizzard. The hero had helped him twice and had pleaded for his powers to be reinstated. He had claimed to hate the Hero Foundation. How could it be him?

A thought struck Jake. Mr Grimm; could it be him? He shook the notion away. Grimm had been there for him when nobody else had. Grimm had openly told him that he worked for both sides. Why would Grimm even put the idea into his head if it were him?

This matter only complicated issues.

A Traitor Within

'My parents are my priority. Are they alive?' His voice trembled.

'The Enforcers took them to a Foundation hospital. They are alive. Barely. It seems Pete manifested a poison. Perhaps something Viral left in the raw powers he absorbed.' Viral had died the same time Pete had obtained his extraordinary powers. It wasn't beyond reason to suspect that his powers may have corrupted Pete's.

'Maybe, but he knew what he was doing. It was a deliberate act.'

'And you want to kill him in revenge?'

'No. You said he can manipulate the powers already inside him. I want him to reverse what he's done—give me an antidote for my parents. But I don't trust him to do it freely. There must be a way to get it out of him.'

Mr Grimm wasn't impressed. 'The old Jake Hunter would be trying to tear him limb from limb.'

'My parents are dying, my sister is trying to kill me, I'm still addicted to the powers from Villain.net, somebody close to me is a traitor and I'm almost halfway through exterminating the Council of Evil—so you could say I have things on my mind.'

'There is a way to get Pete to help you without his consent.' Mr Grimm sat down and studied Jake carefully. 'What do you know about life before the Council of Evil or the Hero Foundation were formed?' Jake

1 0 1 0 0 0 1 1 0 0 1 0 1 0 1 1 1 0 0 1 0 0 1 0 1

shook his head, wondering where this was leading. 'Various heroes had grouped together in an effort to control world events. When Eric Kirby had the idea to create Hero.com he created a team to search for the Origins.'

'The Origins? The origins of what?'

'Of all powers. You see, every power that exists is a spin-off from another power. For example, the power to levitate, glide, and fly all come from the same mutated power. Hurling energy spheres, fireballs, plasma, or lightning . . . they are all cousins of one another. The ultimate powers are called Core Powers. These are the purest form of superpowers. The villain on the loose now, Eon, is altering time. He possesses a Core Power. Only one person alive at any one time can wield a specific Core Power.'

'How does any of this help me?'

'The original team that Kirby led to find the Origins had one important member. He was called Leech.'

'And he could suck other people's powers up?'

'Absorb them, temporarily. Not remove them. He was used to stock up powers for Hero.com, but his true purpose was to find and absorb a Core Power so the team could possess it. If you find Leech then he can help you snatch the poison antidote from inside Pete as well as the power to cure your parents and give them back their memories . . . permanently.'

A Traitor Within

Jake felt his nerves jangle with excitement—Leech's one power could solve all his immediate problems. 'He must be ancient by now. Do you know where he is?'

'He is old and he shunned the heroic path and found his own inner peace. As to where he is I cannot say. But there is somebody who does. One of the most feared Council members and Necros's lieutenant: Armageddon. Leech was his father. He rejected his son when he turned to evil.'

'Armageddon has a dad? Weird. That's like you having one.' Jake noticed Grimm's face flicker. Of course he must have had parents. Maybe that's why he sympathized with Jake's plight? 'So you want me to go up and ask Armageddon for help?'

'I believe the warmonger will be against that idea. You must coerce the information from him.'

'Coerce? You mean torture him?'

Grimm shrugged. 'There are subfolders on Villain.net where you will find the resources you need.'

'Subfolders? What do you mean?'

'Oh, you don't know? I assumed Basilisk had explained everything to you the day he introduced you to the website. For advanced users, such as yourself, there are certain icons on the screen that you can right-click on and enter a subfolder. In there you will find variant powers more suited to *specific* tasks.'

'There appear to be a lot of things I don't know.'

Mr Grimm smiled in response to that. Jake felt it was a rather smug smile.

'Armageddon was on your hit list, so there is no change of plan, we can still bring down the Council of Evil.'

Jake's mind was racing. He couldn't take out Armageddon alone. He needed Munir and Lorna. His hand dug into his pocket as he thought. His fingers touched the two crystal pendants he had taken from the Council leaders. He held them up to the light. They were clear and unremarkable.

'What are these?' He held them to the light for Grimm to see.

'They look like cheap trinkets of no importance. Where did you get them?'

Jake didn't bother answering. He suspected they might be of use at a later date. For now, the clock was ticking and his parents were dying.

Pete returned Momentum's unwavering gaze. He couldn't believe how his fortunes had changed since he woke from the coma. He thought long and hard about Momentum's offer and came to the conclusion that the offer was legitimate.

He was being handed his own army, a group of superpowered malcontents who wanted to use their powers for selfish reasons. A group with no affiliations to either the Council of Evil or the Hero Foundation. Momentum was offering him the leadership of Forge.

Pete could enjoy all the benefits the Council of Evil had to offer—the website, the workshops, scientific research centres, and the excellent gym—and he could lead his own gang. Even better, he would no longer have to work on those stupid missions for Necros.

Momentum told Pete that he had co-created Forge with the express aim of having a fallback should the Council fall. Now that looked likely to happen, Momentum needed somebody to look after the ragtag army.

If Pete had a plan to rob a vault, terrorize a country, or steal anything then he didn't have to go through the Council's bureaucracy to get a permit. He could rally Forge and just do it.

'And there's no strings attached?' Pete asked for the third time.

'Only that ultimate control rests with me if I need to leave this place.' Momentum indicated his own chamber. 'I have no wish to be here when the empire falls. You will lead Forge to great things.'

During his coma, Pete had dreamt of great wealth and commanding supervillains as his own servants, and now he had the chance. Greedy thoughts fuelled his imagination—and why not? He had had very little at home; his parents had struggled to make ends meet.

He paused. That was the first time he had thought about his parents in a long time. When Jake had released him from the hospital, Pete had visited the remains of his home. There was nothing left and his parents had gone. They were separating anyway, but he had no idea where they were now.

Thinking of his parents and Jake brought back the reality of what he had done to Hunter. His mouth went dry at the thought of poisoning Jake's family.

'What about Jake?'

'What about him?'

'How are his parents? Did I . . . did he . . . ?'

'You have done exactly as I asked.'

'But why? I don't understand what it serves by harming them.' Pete had longed to be a villain, and had enjoyed unleashing his darker side. But there was still enough of the innocent boy inside to express concern.

'If I were to threaten to kill your family, how would you feel?'

Pete shrugged. If he was completely honest he didn't care right now.

'It angers Hunter. And I need his anger to boil to the surface, to manifest into something ugly. He may finally be of some use to us.'

A Traitor Within

'But he's already a Council member. What more use can he be?'

'You misunderstand. I don't mean of use to the Council, I mean to *us*, to Forge. Jake Hunter is about to become the greatest weapon we could hope to have. And he doesn't even know it.'

The reunion with Munir and Lorna had not been what Jake was expecting. Munir had leapt to his feet and embraced Jake when he returned to the castle. He had then rapidly summarized what had happened when Jake had left London.

Jake mumbled an explanation of how he had defeated Mobius and why he had hastily departed. He didn't mention Pete, especially with Lorna in earshot; he didn't want her to discover his true nature.

Munir had then excitedly told Jake about how his powers were now more potent than ever. He actually had tears in his eyes when he thanked Jake for restoring them. He didn't act like a sneaky two-faced traitor.

Lorna's behaviour was completely opposite. She had coolly acknowledged Jake's return. He had at least been expecting a hug, instead he got a terse smile. She remained unusually quiet when Jake skimmed over how he had defeated Mobius.

She wasn't acting like a traitor either. Jake had

bullied enough people to recognize somebody who had retreated into their own shell. She was being a typical girl, making him guess what she was thinking.

Then it struck him—he knew what the problem was. She was annoyed with him for abandoning her in London! That must be it. Jake had more important things to worry about than Lorna's feelings. She'd snap out of it.

Jake outlined his plan to bring Armageddon to justice and that they would find him in Baghdad. Munir was enthusiastic; Lorna was unreadable. She only spoke once:

'Is he one of the Council of Evil too? Like Professor Mobius?'

A quick glance at Munir told him who had informed her of the truth. He nodded, uncertain exactly how much Munir had told her. However, they both agreed to accompany him.

'We need to wipe these villains off the map,' said Lorna coolly. 'All of them.'

There was vitriol in her voice, but Jake didn't hear it. He was just relieved to have her support in facing one of the strongest Council members. Even Necros feared the mighty Armageddon.

Jake was eager to leave straight away, but a wave of fatigue overwhelmed him. He was overtired and had to recharge his powers from Villain.net. He found himself recharging more frequently lately, but he would worry about that at a later date.

He headed off for a shower and a sleep. He shouted for Igor, but his servant was nowhere to be found. Jake had a shower then headed for his Command Centre to recharge while he slept. He was alarmed to discover the security door was missing. Somebody had been up in the tower.

A quick inspection revealed nothing was missing. It was as he left it.

Suspicion fought tiredness. Igor: he hadn't thought of the mute when he was making a list of potential traitors—but Igor knew almost everything about Jake and now he was missing.

Jake found he was running back down the stairs before he registered something was wrong. He charged to the lounge, unlocking the door with the key only he and Igor possessed.

Chameleon was gone. There was nothing but a pile of broken crystals. Jake's stomach lurched. His arch-nemesis had broken out. Had Igor helped him? That didn't make sense. When Chameleon had broken into the castle, it was Igor who had attacked him.

'I thought you were going to rest?'

Jake spun round to see Lorna was watching him from the doorway. Jake felt as though he had been caught red-handed, although there was no evidence to make Lorna suspicious.

'I am. I just wanted to check something.'

Lorna walked into the room and looked at the crystal fragments.

'What have you broken?'

'Something of . . . sentimental value.'

'I didn't think you had sentiments,' she snapped before she could stop herself.

Jake was surprised by Lorna's tone. He forced a thin smile. 'Not any more, obviously.'

Lorna managed a smile. 'Sorry, that came out a bit harsh.'

Jake was too tired to think. Chameleon knew the whereabouts of his base, which meant he was no longer safe here, but he was too tired to leave immediately.

'You should grab a couple of hours sleep like you said.'

Jake nodded. Lorna was still acting icy towards him, but he was happy that she wasn't a traitor—or Munir either. Perhaps Igor was, for whatever reason, the traitor. After all, he had vanished without a trace.

'We better make it an hour,' said Jake, eager not to spend any longer than necessary in the compromised headquarters—but equally he couldn't afford to face Armageddon exhausted.

He crossed to the staircase. Lorna called after him.

A Traitor Within

'What was the sentimental item?'

Jake hesitated. This time he didn't have to lie.

'It was a victory statue.'

Beth's vision blurred as the tears came. She wiped them and blew her snotty nose before looking back through the observation window at her parents lying still on parallel beds. Nurses walked around them, dressed in cumbersome biohazard suits. The Foundation doctors were uncertain if the virus that gripped them was contagious or not. They couldn't afford to take any chances.

Beth recalled the day Eric Kirby had visited her in the private school she had attended. The headmaster had taken her into his office and told her Kirby was a very important person.

Of course she hadn't believed Kirby's wild stories of heroes, villains, and superpowers—until he had shown her Hero.com. She was shocked to learn that the villain they called Dark Hunter was out to kill her family. Even with the incredible things she had finally taken as a reality, the fact her family was in any danger seemed implausible.

She had watched footage, taken from an Enforcer helicopter, of a bunch of villains fighting some poor kid in his back garden and trashing his home. The boy was apparently at the local school and didn't live too far away. Then Kirby showed her footage of another house in the neighbourhood that had been flattened by a tornado conjured by a supervillain.

She had been told Dark Hunter was behind both heinous attacks. He was picking off kids and their families in her town. It seemed bizarre, but she couldn't refute the proof.

Now she had seen the results for herself. She had witnessed Dark Hunter trying to kill her parents.

Kirby had told her about the history of heroes, and she understood why they needed new blood.

As she watched her frail parents she wiped away the tears and vowed revenge. Several weeks ago she was an active, intelligent girl who liked hockey and horse riding. It had taken rigorous training, superpowers, and a death threat against her family to turn her into a warrior.

Eric Kirby appeared behind Beth and laid a comforting hand on her shoulder.

'I have some news that may interest you. I know where Dark Hunter will be heading next.'

Beth went rigid at the mere mention of his name.

'Tell me.'

Eric Kirby smiled. He was happy that Jake Hunter, the super-weapon the Council of Evil had lured to their side, would soon be caught and safely stored in a vault. Then the Foundation could continue their experiments where they left off the day Jake had broken from Diablo Island.

Kirby had every faith that Beth wouldn't fail.

'Baghdad,' he said. 'You'll find the Dark Hunter there.'

1
7
0
|
0
|
0
0
0
0
|
0
0
|
0
|
0
|
0
|
|
0
|
0
0
|
0
0
|
|
0
|
|

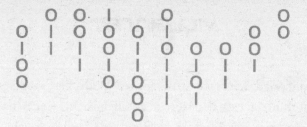

Baghdad

It was unseasonably warm when Jake, Lorna, and Munir teleported into Baghdad. Jake had been expecting a war zone when they arrived, but instead they stepped from a quiet side street into a long wide avenue, covered in a fine layer of sand and alive with a constant stream of traffic. The vehicles looked old, some of them in such poor shape Jake wondered how they kept going.

The buildings were flat roofed and earth coloured, and Jake was surprised to see plush green trees dotting the road. It didn't look too bad. The people who walked the street mostly wore the traditional ankle length dishdasha, a few wore a kaffiyeh to protect their heads. The women wore black abayahs with asha scarves that covered their heads, but not their faces. Everybody seemed happy enough, a far cry from the sorrow shown on TV.

Munir had cautioned Lorna to cover her hair—they might be superpowered, but they should be respectful of other cultures. She opted for a hooded top that

concealed her face in shadows. With her shapeless clothing, a casual observer could take her for a boy. Jake wore his hood up to hide his blond hair, which was very distinctive in a country where dark hair was the norm.

'Where are we going to find this sneak?' asked Jake, referring to the informant Mr Grimm had set up. The informant wanted a large sum of cash for revealing Armageddon's lair.

'The café should be somewhere around here,' said Munir. 'When we get there, neither of you say anything. Leave the talking to me.'

Jake was glad to have Munir with them, he fitted into the city. Not for the first time, Jake was happy to have a sidekick.

They slowly walked down the street, the heat sapping their strength with every step. Munir scanned the Arabic signs until he found what he was looking for. A group of men were sitting outside, drinking and smoking. They eyed the three strangers suspiciously.

After a brief exchange in Arabic, they were allowed to enter.

The café was dark inside, and cloying smoke hugged the rafters. Ceiling fans pushed the smoke around and did little to cool the humid atmosphere. The room was packed with more people smoking and playing chess. Despite the civilized gaming, there was an air of menace to the room. The players all looked fierce and battle-hardened, and they were all armed. Most had pistols visible; others had AK-47s propped against the table. Even with his superpowers, Jake suddenly felt unsafe.

Munir talked quietly to the barman and was shown a far table where a young man was sitting, focused on the game in front of him. An old bearded man sat opposite and quickly moved away when Munir introduced himself, but the young man only looked up when Munir switched to English.

'Take a seat,' said the man and gestured for Jake and Lorna to join them. 'English is my preferred tongue.' He looked around the room with weaselly eyes. 'And some of the louts here are not to be trusted but fortunately don't speak English very well. My name is Adil. Please, have some tea.'

Jake's illusions of the tough uncivilized country were derailed when Adil poured them all tea from a pot at the side of his table.

'Do you play?' Adil asked Jake, pointing to the table.

'My dad tried to teach me chess when I was younger. Didn't get the hang of it.'

'This is not chess it is shatranj. Think of it as the grandfather to chess as you know it now. It's a game of skill, intellect, and cunning.' His eyes bored into Jake. 'It teaches strategy by encouraging imagination.

For somebody in your position, I would think they were crucial skills. It is always important to be one step ahead of your rival, and to plan your moves in advance.'

'You don't know me,' Jake snapped back. He was feeling on edge, and had no time to listen to preaching fools.

'I know what you want, and why. Our mutual friend was very clear about the urgency of the matter. The villain you seek has been causing us trouble for many years with his violence and extortion. He won't be missed.'

'Then stop stalling and take us to him,' growled Jake. The thick smoke was starting to dry his throat so he downed the lukewarm tea and thumped the cup back on the table.

'How I miss the impetuousness of youth,' retorted Adil. It was clear he wasn't going to be rushed. 'I risk a lot for displeasing Armageddon. He controls the underground world here. Everybody fears him. You have my compensation?'

'Three hundred thousand dollars was wired to your account the moment we sat down,' said Munir coolly.

Adil checked his mobile phone. A few moments later and he was satisfied.

'So I see. Then it is my turn to keep my end of

the bargain. But first I need to make sure you know what you are doing. Why do you seek him out, Hunter?'

'He has something I want.'

'It must be something very precious.'

There was a greedy glimmer in Adil's eye. Jake didn't reply. When Adil realized that no answer was forthcoming, he simply nodded and stood up.

'Come.' He strode out of the café.

Jake swapped glances with Munir and Lorna who both looked tense. As they followed Adil, Jake was aware the man carried no visible weapon. Was he a Downloader . . . or even a Prime?

Outside, they were led to a battered Toyota pickup truck in a side street. They climbed inside. Adil had only just shut the doors when the vehicle shook and five heavily armed figures clambered on the back. Jake peered through the narrow rear window and caught glimpses of AK-47s and rocket launchers.

'Who are they?' he asked with concern.

'My entourage,' was Adil's cool reply. They pulled into the main avenue at a surprising turn of speed. Under the battered pickup's bonnet, the engine sounded remarkably well maintained.

Their guide remained silent as they headed through the heart of Baghdad. As the buildings grew in size, so did the signs of war. In places, bomb craters were still

filled with dirty water; some buildings were black and charred where fires had gutted them.

Occasional Iraqi security vehicles passed by, but paid them no heed. Jake glanced behind to check the men in the back were not waving their weapons in the air. They looked like a bunch of labourers on their way to work.

They crossed the River Tigris, passing a statue of a military figure. For the first time Adil spoke up.

'We are now in Karkh, the west side of the river. That statue is of Adnan Khairallah, the brother-in-law of our notorious ex-dictator. Khairallah is still something of a local hero to the people here.'

No further snippets of tourism information were forthcoming. Jake noticed an increase in Government security. Adil wisely kept away from those areas.

'That's the Green Zone,' said Munir. 'The most secure part of the city. We won't find our friend there.'

They passed an airport to the south, and continued through the suburbs for over an hour in silence. The beige streets continued with monotonous regularity, power lines zigzagging from building to building. The occasional blue and yellow mosque broke the colour scheme. Towards the suburbs there was a distinct air of poverty. Lorna was sad to see many children, some her own age, sitting forlornly on the pavement.

Baghdad

The surrounding desert sands were becoming more apparent along the side of the road and Jake was surprised again when the monotone buildings were replaced by verdant fields that were irrigated by another broad river: the Euphrates.

'How much further?' asked Jake. He was feeling irritable, cooped up inside the hot vehicle. They could have flown here in minutes instead of roughing it.

Adil pointed ahead. The world's most battered car ferry was waiting for them. The pickup rolled onto a rusting metal deck. Black diesel fumes poured from the ferry's engine as they crossed the river. Jake thought it was painfully slow and was starting to get impatient. Sparks flickered between his fingers. Munir gave a quick shake of the head—the meaning was clear: don't start any trouble.

On the other side of the river, they drove for another thirty minutes until the landscape opened up into a spectacular desert vista. The sands looked like a golden ocean. Adil stopped the car.

'Out,' he barked.

Munir frowned. 'What? Here?'

Jake was eager to leave the car. Munir looked suspiciously around. Lorna grabbed Jake's arm and he felt her nails dig in.

'I don't like the look of this.'

Jake followed her gaze to the five thugs who had

dismounted from the pickup and now had an assortment of rifles and rocket launchers aimed at them.

'You traitor!' snarled Munir.

Adil shrugged. 'To be a traitor I must have something to believe in order to betray it. I know what you're all capable of, but rest assured my men have dealt with Supers before. If you attack they will kill at least one of you before they fall.'

'We paid you!' said Jake through clenched teeth.

'A welcome donation, I assure you. Please understand, Armageddon is a most powerful adversary and I do not think you have what it takes to defeat him. If you did, then I would be more than happy to let the tyrant be killed. If you fail your assassination then I will be held to account by him. So answer me this, why should I be placing my life on the line for you?'

The temperature wasn't helping Jake's temper.

'Grimm said you could be trusted!' snarled Jake. His fists were beginning to glow with radioactive rage. The gunmen licked their lips and gripped their weapons tighter. 'I don't have time for games! Take us to where we asked, or pay the consequences.'

Adil sneered. 'What consequences, boy?'

Jake's movement was a blur. He fired a fizzling radioactive cord at Adil, hurling him against the pickup. Jake's other hand extended towards the nearest rifle-toting thug. Concentric energy circles radiated out, encapsulating the man in a glowing veil of energy. He dropped to his knees screaming.

The four other gunmen pulled their triggers to fire. Jake's eyes were red. He roared with fury—the gunmen's weapons melted in their hands before the bullets could leave the chamber. They screamed as they dropped the liquefied weapons, then turned and fled in the pickup.

Adil looked at the smoking hole in his robes. The raw flesh beneath quickly healed, and he met Jake's gaze with a smile.

'Not bad.'

Jake gulped deep breaths to calm down. He heard Lorna gasp, she had never seen Jake lose his temper before.

Adil's eyes widened. 'You truly are as powerful as I have heard!' Adil extended his hand. 'You have proved yourself to me. Now I believe Armageddon can be toppled.'

Munir spat on the ground. 'That was a test?'

'Yes. If I am to risk my life, then I need to know those I fight with are as capable as they claim. It was a necessary deception.' He held Jake's gaze, his hand still extended. 'It will be an honour to fight with you.'

Jake reluctantly shook his hand. When Adil tried to pull away, Jake increased his grip.

'Time is running out. Stall one more time and I won't hesitate to kill you.'

Adil flinched as Jake increased the pressure and bones cracked in his hand. Adil pulled his hand free. The bones were crushed and limp. He shook it and the hand appeared to pop back into shape.

'I understand. Armageddon's fortress is not far. It's over those dunes. We can fly now if you prefer.'

'What about him?' asked Lorna, pointing to the man who was still jerking in his own world of pain.

Without hesitation, intense blue flames erupted from Adil's mouth. In seconds the injured thug was nothing but a pile of ashes. Adil met Lorna's stunned gaze; she had seen a lot of terrible things since she became a superhero, but she'd never seen anybody act with such callousness—even the supervillains she had encountered.

'An unfortunate casualty of war. Let us go.'

Adil led Jake's team in a short flight across to a high ridge of dunes. A mile beyond lay the sprawling ruins dating back to the Ottoman Empire. The desert winds had ripped off rooftops, but many of the stone pillars and walls still stood.

Jake was deeply unimpressed. Even his lair was better.

'Do not be deceived. All is not what it seems. The lair is cloaked to keep away the unwary.'

'Or this could be another ambush you're setting up,' growled Munir.

Adil ignored the provocation. He closed his eyes and extended his hand. Electricity leapt from his fingers, except the snaking charges moved sluggishly across the ground. It was like watching lightning in extreme slow motion.

The electricity skirted around the rocks and fallen stone blocks before it and suddenly struck an invisible shield. A translucent dome flickered around the ruins and new buildings suddenly became visible. At first they rippled like a mirage, then became solid. Black metal spires, covered in satellite dishes, and jagged towers absorbed the sunlight. They spiralled from the ground like twisted roots. Jake instantly recognized the design ethos as the same Armageddon used for his armour.

Munir studied the complex with a practised eye. 'I can't see any guards.'

'Rest assured, there are,' said Adil.

'What's the best way in?' asked Lorna.

'The only way in is through the main door. Fear not, Armageddon isn't known for shying away from fights. We shall find him easily enough.'

They boldly approached an open plaza. A large pair of blast doors, big enough to swallow an aircraft, blocked their way. As they approached the doors opened with a rumble.

'It appears that we're expected,' whispered Lorna. 'I wonder who tipped him off?'

Although she hadn't mentioned the word 'traitor', the thought rattled Jake. He tried to put it out of his mind.

They entered a large spacious room, more like a hangar. It was lit by red lights so defining detail was impossible. Their echoing footsteps had a metallic ring.

Jake suddenly caught movement either side of them. At first he thought giant spiders were attacking them, until his eyes adjusted and he realized they were three metre tall mechanized insects. The front of the machines looked like ugly robotic insect heads. A pair of glowing red bug-eyes studied the intruders. A single cannon, the size of Jake, was mounted on their backs.

The insectoids came to a halt, but didn't attack—they just watched him. Jake's hackles rose. His enemy was close.

'I know you're here, Armageddon,' taunted Jake. 'Are you too scared to show yourself?'

A crimson spotlight suddenly shone down at the far end of the room, revealing Armageddon seated on an elaborate throne.

His large crowned head swept upwards. Although his eyes were hidden behind a mask, they all had a sense he was staring at them. His four muscular arms tensed as his fists bunched.

Armageddon's voice boomed around the chamber like thunder. 'The Dark Hunter, I should have known it was you who would betray the Council of Evil.'

Out of the corner of his eye, he saw Lorna go rigid. Jake's stomach churned—he had been thoughtless to engage in a conversation that would reveal everything he wanted to conceal from Lorna. It was too late to change things now, he would have to sort it out later.

Armageddon continued: 'I told Necros that it was an inside job, run by a traitorous wretch like you, but he would rather believe otherwise.'

So Necros still believed he was one of the team? That was useful to know. Jake's mind raced. So far he had not displayed any aggression. He thought of Adil's comment about strategy. Perhaps now was not the time to fight Armageddon? Perhaps he would willingly volunteer the information he needed.

'I came here for your help.'

Armageddon leaned forward, and Jake could now see the baneful red eyes staring at him.

The fiend gave a wheezy laugh. 'My help?'

'My parents are dying. I need to find Leech and since he left the Foundation, it appears that you're the only one who knows where he is.'

At the mention of his father's name, Armageddon

strode forward. Each footfall was like an elephant step. He circled around Jake's crew. The sound of the villain's armour plates sliding across his joints was like scissors.

'And if I refuse?'

'My parents will die.'

'That is not a convincing argument, Hunter. You know who Leech really is.'

'Your father.'

'Then you should know I would not expose him to somebody like you.'

Jake was having a hard time believing somebody as vile and hated as Armageddon was getting defensive about his own father. Jake felt the familiar rush of anger. He had been a fool to think he could talk his way through the problem. His old bullying instinct took over his mouth.

'I don't have time to play around. Tell me how to find Leech or I will force it from you.'

Armageddon's laugh sounded like a violent lightning strike.

'You and your super-team? Better people have faced me. All have failed. Your threats are—'

Jake's temper had been steadily rising. He felt his face flush red and he instinctively extended both hands. Beams of light shot from both of them hitting Armageddon with Herculean force. The villain was flung across the chamber—tearing his throne in half as he bounced off it.

Munir had sensed Jake was coiled to strike. He fired an ice blast into the nearest mechanical beast. The insectoid froze solid, vapour rising from it. He followed the attack with a spin-kick—shattering the now brittle machine into dust.

The second mech fired a blue orb of energy that sent Lorna and Adil sprawling across the floor.

Jake watched as Lorna slid past him—breaking his focused concentration on the Council member. Jake flew across to where Lorna had hit the wall. He helped her up—

Lorna punched him hard across the face. Jake was stunned, and it wasn't even a super-punch. She had tears in her eyes.

'Why did you lie to me?' Lorna was breaking apart, unable to hide what she knew about Jake. 'I know about you, Jake. I know what you have done!'

'Lorna, I didn't . . . I mean, I—'

An ice wall suddenly arced over their heads as two more mechs scuttled across the ceiling, firing down on them. Chunks of the wall shattered from the impact. Munir skated across to them—firing icicles into one of the machines.

'This is no time for a marital barney!' he screamed. 'Get it together!'

Lorna wiped the tears from her eyes—then suddenly kicked Jake in the chest. It was powerful enough to topple him onto his back.

Before Jake could shout at her, Armageddon's blast passed through the air where he had been standing and struck Lorna.

Jake was distraught as he watched the flesh rip from half her face—it was like looking at an X-ray. Lorna's limp body spun into the shadows.

'NO! Lorn!' he screamed, his voice breaking with emotion.

'Jake!' screamed Munir. 'He's getting up!'

Jake turned to see Armageddon advancing. His armour was dented from where Jake had attacked him. Jake's vision blurred and he felt a wave of dizziness overcome him. He was now more than angry. His vision turned red, his eyes glowing like hot coals. He didn't dare see if Lorna was still alive—that was a question he didn't want answering right now.

Four swords appeared in Armageddon's hands, placed there by an intricate mechanism springing them from his arm. He spun the four blades like a samurai warrior.

Jake charged forward like a raging bull. Four insectoids dropped from the ceiling to block his path. Adil spat fire at them all, turning them into scrap before they hit the floor.

Baghdad

Armageddon whirled his blades so quickly they looked like a solid shield. Jake hit the spinning blades. One of the swords shattered from the impact, he felt another bite deep into his shoulder. Jake staggered back but kept his balance. He shot a fireball at the villain. Armageddon slugged the ball of flames aside—inadvertently frying another mech that had been ready to join in the fight.

The whirling blades advanced again. Two swords gouged the floor—the third stabbed through Jake's stomach, clanging on the wall behind him. Jake gasped, and found his mouth was suddenly filled with blood. Already his healing power was knitting the skin around the sword.

Armageddon leant close to gloat.

'It hurts, doesn't it?'

Without thinking, Jake tensed and invoked his lightning power—except he focused it internally. Three million volts surged through the sword and flung Armageddon against the wall, leaving the sword stuck in Jake.

Jake winced as he gripped the blade and slowly slid it out, reopening the wound. It was agony, but eventually the weapon fell to the floor. He spat out a mouthful of blood and raised his fists, ready to strike again.

Armageddon's armour was still smouldering, and his breath came in asthmatic wheezes. With a dexterous flip, the three remaining swords tucked back into his arms. The villain charged towards Jake.

Jake bellowed and ran towards Armageddon as fast as he could. He had no plan. He was working off pure instinct.

As the two titans were about to impact, Armageddon suddenly rolled into an armoured ball. He hurtled into Jake, and, rather than bounce off, Jake found himself snagged on the serrated edges of the villain's armour and crushed as Armageddon rolled over him multiple times.

Both Council members crashed through the wall with unbelievable force, tearing a ragged hole in the steel and rolling into the desert sands outside. The impact forced Armageddon out of his ball and Jake landed on top of the fiend who was twice his size.

Jake needed the information from Armageddon in a hurry, so he didn't have time to talk. He concentrated on accessing the subfolder powers Mr Grimm had told him to download. The hidden folder he found on Villain.net had taken Jake to a whole new screen where the icons used to describe the powers were gorily graphic.

Jake concentrated on thinking about those powers he had absorbed. Like searching through fog, they materialized in his thoughts. Like all powers, they came with a telepathic set of instructions: just by accessing the power he instantly knew how to control it.

Jake pressed his fingers against Armageddon's armour—the metal sizzled from the pressure until his fingers fell through to the flesh beneath. Jake couldn't see what was happening, but he could feel his own fingertips wriggle like worms as they pierced the villain's skin. There they would drive down to his nerves, allowing Jake to administer mind-numbing pain. Armageddon's entire body jerked.

With a lion-like roar, Armageddon freed a hand and punched Jake off him.

Jake soared through the air—his back cracking as he toppled an ancient pillar.

'You fool!' Armageddon roared. 'I am unbeatable! I am too powerful! I am your end of days!'

Jake didn't care about the threats. He was far too mad. His healing factor was working too slowly for his liking. Jake staggered to his feet.

Armageddon was ready for him. He lunged forward—stamping one foot hard against the ground. Jake felt a seismic tremble and a crack opened in the ground, heading straight for him. He leapt aside—but Armageddon stamped again. More cracks radiated out at incredible speed.

Jake hovered in the air and laughed. 'Is that all you've got?'

Armageddon snarled and raised all four arms to the heavens. A strong wind picked up and the sky darkened. Jake looked around to see what the new threat was.

Walls of dust rose on every horizon. Adil leapt through the hole in the wall and instantly took in the situation.

'He's summoning a haboob—a sandstorm!'

Jake fired his radioactive blast at Armageddon—it didn't even faze the villain. His armour absorbed the crackling radiation and glowed. Adil spat a fireball at Armageddon—it did nothing.

Before they could do any more, the sandstorm was upon them. Jake closed his eyes tight. The storm roared in his ear and his skin felt as if it was being attacked with sandpaper. He thought he heard Adil scream, but it was swallowed by the rumbling.

The pain was intense, and Jake's healing power was having trouble constantly coping with replacing his skin. Jake staggered blindly into a wall, getting more furious with every step.

'No!' he screamed—instantly getting a mouthful of sand.

His anger manifested a new power. A wave of air suddenly shot from his body—instantly repelling the mighty sandstorm. Armageddon looked around in astonishment as the dust scattered.

'How did you do that?'

'You'll find I'm full of surprises.' Jake's voice was lost in a dry hacking cough as he spat out sand, thankful that his unusually fast healing ability had prevented him from being torn apart. He noticed a skeleton lying half submerged in the sand. The scraps of clothing that clung to the bleached bones indicated it was Adil—he'd been literally sandblasted apart; his powers had been too slow to mend the damage.

Jake's glowing eyes bore into his enemy. Multiple powers sloshed inside his system, mixing and mutating in ways scientists had been trying to master for decades.

His thinking was suddenly crystal clear. He had been a fool. He didn't have to take the Council out one at a time. They were afraid of him: they knew he could take them all out if he tried. By containing his anger he had weakened himself, smothered his real potential.

Rage was what propelled him through life. He felt a sudden surge of power. His wrath was his saviour.

Armageddon hurled a ball of cobalt energy at him. It glanced on Jake's side, but he barely noticed. He looked like a zombie as his regeneration powers battled to heal him up. He could feel chunks of flesh hanging from his arms and body. His ear felt funny, and a quick check revealed it wasn't in fact there any more. His regeneration powers would heal him whole, but it was his rage that made him stand. He swiped his hand as if swatting a fly.

The sands next to Armageddon suddenly ripped up into a huge octopus-like tentacle that wrapped around the villain—the sand-tentacle's movements mirrored Jake's hand.

The villain screamed as the sand-limb crushed around his midriff, pinning all four arms to his side. It plucked him off his feet and suspended him in front of Jake.

'I'm not going to ask you where your father is. I'm going to force you to tell me.'

He tugged at Armageddon's helmet. It didn't budge. He grasped it firmly and accelerated straight up—metal tore and the helmet gave way with an asthmatic hiss. He flung it aside. The face that greeted him was of a thin, white-haired man in his early fifties. He looked frail, kept alive by a dozen pipes plumbed into his throat. He noticed a pendant around the villain's neck. It was the same as the others he had stolen from the Council leaders. He ripped it off.

'What is this?'

Armageddon gasped for breath. There were no answers there. Jake pushed his hand into Armageddon's head. His fingers melted through the skin—and the villain howled. Jake called up another of his subfolder interrogation powers and stabbed his fingers into

Baghdad

Armageddon's brain. It felt as if he was shoving his fingers into thick, warm porridge.

Jake's mind was suddenly full of flickering images, as Armageddon's memories became his. It felt like watching a thousand films in seconds. The whole experience was overwhelming, and Jake thought his head might explode. He concentrated, narrowing down the torrent of information to just what he needed.

Then it came to him—flickering images of his father rejecting his villainous son. The anguish drove Armageddon on to become a member of the Council. The pictures and meaning were vague and scrambled. Jake got some of the meaning—the Foundation had stashed Leech beyond the reach of his son. Armageddon didn't know where he was.

Jake was confused—why had Grimm told him he would know?

Jake slid his fingers away and reeled backwards. He felt crushed because he had failed to find Leech. He also had a nagging sense of suspicion. Had he been deliberately set up to eradicate the super-fiend, or was Grimm's information simply wrong?

The sand-tentacle was still crushing Armageddon, but the villain was forcing his last laugh. A dial on his chest was flashing; an ominous tone was increasing in pitch. Jake knew Armageddon wasn't going to go down without fighting. The villain had triggered a nuclear bomb built into his suit. He was going to take the entire area out!

The sand tentacle kept Armageddon pinned down. There was nothing Jake could do to diffuse the bomb, he had to get away.

'Lorn!' The thought of Lorna and Munir galvanized Jake back inside the fortress. He couldn't leave them there.

The sudden change from bright desert to dim room didn't help his vision.

'Lorna? Munir? Where are you guys?'

He ran across to where he last saw Lorna. She wasn't there, only a patch of blood remained. He hoped Munir had teleported them both out so he could get Lorna some medical attention. If she was still alive.

Jake was concentrating on teleporting away, when a familiar voice spoke up.

'You're not going anywhere, Hunter!'

He turned to see Beth hanging upside-down from the ceiling. She acrobatically dropped to the floor.

'You tried to kill my parents, so I have no qualms about hurting you,' she snarled.

'Beth, you've got to listen to me, there's a nuclear bomb about to go off any moment now. We have to go!'

Beth laughed. 'Yeah, right. You're not going any-where.'

Baghdad

With a sinking feeling he knew she was right. His sister was neutralizing his teleport power. If he didn't think of something fast, the atomic explosion would vaporize them both.

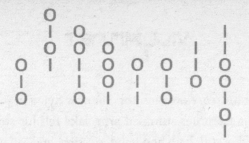

The Road to Recovery

The tone of the bomb continued rising. Jake was painfully aware the next beep might be the last thing he ever heard. He had to get away—and he had to get Beth to follow him. She had been assisting their parents the last time he escaped her clutches, so she hadn't seen the SkyByke and he saw no reason why the same trick wouldn't work.

He thumbed his remote key fob.

The SkyByke appeared with a loud bang, momentarily distracting Beth. He leapt aboard and twisted the throttle. He shot through the hole in the wall—ramping over Armageddon, who was held immobile by the sand tentacle. The orb wheels had no problem gaining traction on the soft sand.

He crested a dune—the motorcycle leaping like a salmon as the sand beneath him exploded from an assault from Beth. More fiery missiles streaked past. Fortunately, all were wide. Jake caught a glimpse of

Beth in his rearview monitor. She was flying in pursuit, shooting from her stumped arm. Jake felt his stomach lurch, she still had her hand missing and it was his fault.

The mighty engine in the SkyByke kept him in the lead as he jumped sand dunes like a motocross rider. Beth was still trailing, but he had the edge with his speed.

Several more dunes were jumped at speed. Ahead, Jake could see the Euphrates and the fertile fields beyond. In his imagination he could hear the deadly tone of the nuclear warning escalating. It was time to engage his secret weapon. He thumbed the turbo boost.

While still airborne, small rocket thrusters snapped out of the SkyByke's rear chassis and ignited with fierce blue flames. Jake felt the sudden tug of G-force as the bike accelerated like a missile. The sand below cut in a v-shaped wake. In seconds he was over the river and roaring across the fields. Ahead he could see Baghdad—and it suddenly occurred to him that a missile-shaped object flying over the city might be mis-construed.

He glanced in the rearview monitor and saw that Beth had stopped shooting at him; instead she was placing all her energy in trying to keep up. Thirty seconds later they were over the city. Jake glanced in his monitor in time to see the image whiteout. When the camera recovered he could see a mushroom cloud puncturing the sky.

The nuke was a low yield device, and the city was too far to be directly affected by the wall of fire that vaporized Armageddon's base. Half the fields on the edge of the river were turned to cinders. A wall of air smashed every window in the suburbs. Beth was hit by the sudden turbulence and ricocheted from several buildings.

Jake's SkyByke shook violently. Inside, he couldn't tear his eyes from the mushroom cloud on the monitor.

'Whoooaaaa!!' he screamed as the invisible EMP—Electromagnetic Pulse—generated by the explosion fried the electrical systems on his SkyByke. The rockets extinguished and the vehicle bellyflopped into the street below. The SkyByke tore through power cables that snaked across the street. There would have been sparks if the EMP hadn't put the local power station out of action as well. The cables tangled around the bike as it landed.

The mighty wheels of his ride absorbed the impact, but the bodywork dented and cracked around Jake like an egg. Jake was moving at such speed that the SkyByke wobbled precariously as he fought for control. It bounced off several other vehicles that had suddenly rolled to a standstill as their engines died. Jake managed to pull the bike in a side-skid—but because the

spherical wheels had been designed to take him around corners at impossible speeds, the skid did little to slow him down.

However, the building in front of him did. Jake slewed into a wall with such force the concrete cracked across the façade. The SkyByke toppled over, spilling a cut and bruised Jake to the floor.

The crowd of spectators didn't pay him any heed. They were all staring at the mushroom cloud on the horizon, wondering what new horror it foretold. They didn't realize that the boy who fell from the sky had just eradicated a supervillain who had been keeping the city under his yoke of terror.

Jake glanced at the cuts on his hand. Normally the wound would heal as though it had never been there, but now his skin was violently bubbling and hissing as it healed. Something wasn't right.

Further thoughts were curtailed by gasps from the crowd as Beth landed amongst them. She must have sustained damage from the explosion because the edges of her costume were charred.

Jake sagged, so much for getting away from his sister. He would have to fight her.

Beth moved so quickly that Jake didn't even see her do it. He was hoisted over her head and hurled at yet another wall. He crumpled into it, leaving a Jake-sized imprint.

The Road to Recovery

'What did you do to my parents?'

Jake tasted blood in his mouth again. It was really turning out to be a bad day.

'Beth, it wasn't me.'

'Don't you dare use my name!' she snarled. 'I am the Reaper!'

'You're my sister!' Jake blinked and in seconds she had crossed the street and was at his side.

A sizeable crowd had gathered, keeping a wary distance, as Beth flung Jake across the wide street. He collided with the third storey of a building, before dropping flat on his face.

Jake's anger was at boiling point, but he dared not blindly unleash it at his sister.

'It wasn't me. It was Pete . . . ' He tried to stand, but felt unusually weak.

Beth was suddenly over him again. Jake had had enough. He unleashed a fireball. He wanted a tennis ball sized globule of fire, just enough to knock his rampaging sister down.

Instead a huge ball of black flames shot from his palm.

The fireball enveloped Beth and carried her through one building, including two interior walls, before dropping her into the street beyond. She lay motionless.

Jake slowly stood up and stared at his hand. Black flames danced from his fingertips.

'What's happening?' he muttered, horrified.

The crowd around him moved steadily backwards. Nobody wanted to get involved.

Beth stirred. She must have been unconscious for a moment. Jake turned on his heels and ran—he stumbled—and when he caught his balance he was surprised to discover that he was flying.

Jake hovered, trying to rationalize why Beth was no longer blocking his flight powers. The EMP—of course! Jake hadn't paid any attention at school but he had played enough computer games to figure out what was happening. Beth's snag-net would have been electronic; the EMP would have destroyed it, which meant Jake could easily escape.

He hesitated. Now he had no reason to run away from Beth, perhaps he could talk things out with her?

Jake swooped over his sister. A crowd of curious spectators were closing in on her. They fled in terror as Jake dropped from the sky, black flames dripping from his hands for added effect. He shook his hands, extinguishing the fire, then knelt next to his sister.

'Beth?' he said softly. 'Can you hear me?'

Her eyes were unfocused. She was clutching her stomach with her one good hand. His blast had melted her costume to her skin. Once again, Jake felt a terrible wave of guilt.

The Road to Recovery

'Beth . . . I'm sorry. I know you don't remember me, but I am your brother. I didn't try to kill your . . . our parents. I was trying to restore their memories but I was tricked. I know how to do it properly now. I can make us a family again.'

Beth stared at him with blurry eyes. She mumbled something incoherent.

'The Hero Foundation are using you. You're nothing but a weapon to them. An instrument to use against me.'

Beth feebly tried to bat Jake away. She was in a bad condition and showed no signs of healing. Maybe her downloaded powers had worn off. Jake didn't know what to do. He couldn't take her back to the Council of Evil. With increased transit restrictions in place after Amy's assassination he couldn't sneak her in. And if the Council members found her they would certainly kill her. And his castle had no real medical facilities. If he hooked her up to Villain.net and pumped a healing power into her, there was no telling what would happen mixing the two rival website powers together. But he couldn't leave her on the dusty road. He scooped her up in his arms.

'I need to get you out of here.'

A voice suddenly boomed through a loudhailer.

'You on the ground—don't move!'

Jake had been so engrossed in talking to his sister that he hadn't heard the soldiers approach. There were two dozen of them, all wearing bright red and blue radiation suits emblazoned with Coalition insignia and they were all armed with M16s pointed directly at him.

One of the soldiers carried a small Geiger-counter, which he pointed at Jake. The distinctive clicking noise increased.

Jake realized that he and Beth were radioactive. But to what level, he couldn't deduce. That explained why his fireball was not only powerful, but an unusual colour and why his healing powers weren't working properly.

'Put the girl down!' boomed the voice.

The speaker must be hidden in one of the four desert-camouflaged Humvees. A pair of Blackhawk helicopters suddenly roared overhead, the down-draught from the rotors turning the street into a minia-ture sandstorm.

Jake sneered at the surrounding forces. If he hadn't been cradling his injured sister he would have taken them all out, out of spite. However, Beth wasn't healing so he couldn't risk a stray bullet striking her.

Jake teleported out of the danger zone.

The soldiers watched in amazement as Jake faded away . . . then reappeared, looking thoroughly bewil-dered.

Why hadn't they escaped? Beth's snag-net was out of

The Road to Recovery

action and he had momentarily appeared at his destination—only to be dragged back here. Had the radiation mucked up all his powers?

The soldiers were becoming restless with Jake's hesitation.

'One more warning! Put the girl down!'

They must know Beth was on their side otherwise they would have opened fire already. That meant there was still a chance for escape.

Jake took it.

He ran through the hole Beth had made in the house, running back into the street beyond. He ran past his now useless SkyByke. That simple manoeuvre lost the foot soldiers and the Humvees—but not the choppers.

The two Blackhawks effortlessly banked after him. Jake ran and leapt into the air—his planned flight turned into nothing more than a super-leap over another block of buildings. He reached the zenith of his flight and landed on the flat-roofed apartment block. He ran to the other side and glided into the street beyond. He cursed his luck, Beth was too much of a weight to fly with.

The helicopters gave chase. The ground next to Jake was ripped apart by gunfire—so much for protecting the girl! They must have decided killing Jake was more important.

Jake sprinted for a narrow alleyway. The choppers followed overhead, but kicked up too much dust for them to be able to track his movements. He doubled-back and took cover under an elaborate awning held up by stone pillars.

He couldn't fly, he couldn't teleport—his powers were not behaving properly. He was going to have to play smart.

Jake ran away from the sound of the choppers. He turned a corner as the Humvees powered into the street. They must have spotted him because they accelerated towards him.

He turned another corner. Ahead was a busy market. Crowds of people moved amongst stalls selling a variety of local produce. He pushed through the crowd, using just enough of his enhanced strength to push people aside, but not to cause too much of a scene.

The Humvees screeched to a halt at the market entrance. The throng of people prevented them from passing. The helicopters appeared overhead. From above, it was easy to track Jake's progress through the crowd.

Jake dived under a table, ignoring the irate stall-holder. He dragged Beth by her jacket collar as he nipped between stalls. Now it was impossible to track him from above.

The Road to Recovery

A pile of crates stank of fish, but offered more than enough cover to hide. Jake hauled Beth behind them. He cast his eye over her. Her condition had deteriorated. Her eyes were closed and her forehead was damp with fevered perspiration.

'Hold on, Bee,' he said, using a pet name he hadn't uttered since he had been very young. 'Hold in there. I'll get you help.'

He looked through the slits in the crates. Soldiers were pushing their way through the crowds towards him. Some locals were pointing fingers in his general direction and he became aware that the helicopters were hovering. He berated himself; they would have some form of heat seeking cameras. What was he thinking by trying to hide?

He tried to weigh up his options. He couldn't teleport, but that didn't mean he had exhausted all his transport options. Once again he had let his anger cloud the most obvious solution.

The soldiers fanned around the crates, weapons ready. Two of them edged forward and booted the crates over—in time to see the back of Jake disappear through a shimmering quantum tunnel.

Jake appeared on a snow-covered lawn, a stark contrast to the desert clime he had just stepped from. He dropped Beth in the snow and turned to close the portal.

Bullets whizzed through, striking the snow-laden tree branches behind him. Jake motioned to close the portal—but not before a gun-toting soldier charged forward. Jake felt two bullets strike his leg and left arm.

The portal spiralled closed—slicing the barrel of the automatic weapon in two. Jake clutched his leg as bloodstains spattered the snow. His skin fizzled as it closed over the bullet. Jake noticed the bullets were not being forced out like his old healing power had done, they were still inside him—and still hurting. Jake ignored the pain and scooped up his sister.

He staggered across the grounds towards the red-brick hospital building in front of him. It was the only place he knew Beth could be treated properly.

He limped through the double doors and the matronly duty nurse stared at him for moment—before the automatic biometric security recognized him and sounded the alarms.

Jake didn't react as blast doors clanged shut behind him and armed Enforcers surrounded him.

'My sister needs urgent help,' he said to the old man walking slowly towards him, wearing a look of utter surprise. Jake held the man's gaze. 'You did this to her. You better fix her,' he snapped.

Eric Kirby nodded and indicated to a trolley.

The Road to Recovery

As soon as Jake laid Beth down she was whisked away by nurses and orderlies.

Jake looked around the Foundation hospital, measuring the level of security. He'd had no choice but to bring Beth here.

And now he was trapped in enemy territory.

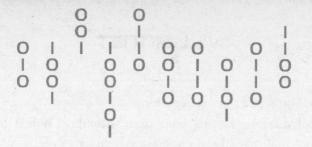

Captured

A platoon of Enforcers marshalled Jake from the hospital. Eric Kirby led them across the grounds towards a strange tank-like vehicle that was pulling up on the lawn. Jake had been forced to control his temper and not put up a fight, the last thing he wanted to do was destroy the hospital his sister was being treated in. His hands were bound behind his back and a belt was strapped to his waist. The buckle was a circular red light that pulsed rhythmically. Kirby had told him it was a snag-net. Jake would be unable to use any of his powers as the device snagged and stored them the second he tried to use them.

'Where are you taking me?'

'A secure facility,' answered Kirby with a note of satisfaction. 'One where we can continue where we left off at Diablo Island.'

Jake's blood boiled. Chameleon had run tests on him during his time at Diablo Island. The Foundation was eager to examine how Jake's powers worked since he had essentially become part of Villain.net.

'You won't discover anything.'

'I disagree. During your time with the Council of Evil they have been studying you most carefully. We were lucky enough to obtain some of their data.'

'The Council didn't study me. They treated me like an equal!'

Kirby whirled round and faced Jake. There was anger in his eyes.

'You're not an equal. You're not a Prime like I am . . . like they are! You use Villain.net to download power to keep you alive. Every time you do that the Council has a team watching and analysing you.'

As much as he hated Kirby, there was a note of truth in his voice.

'That's impossible!'

'Is it? You used the powers directly from the Council's intranet rather than through the website. Each time you were injecting nanobots into your system: microscopic machines designed by them to examine your body and unravel your DNA to discover how you are able to manufacture your powers—which is why your body is reacting oddly after Iraq. It wasn't the radiation, it was the electromagnetic pulse reacting to the nanobots inside you.'

'Why me? I'm not the only one. What about Pete? Why don't you tear him apart and leave me alone?'

Kirby winced at the name. 'Pete is different. He can

only use the powers his body absorbed. True, he has
unique and strange ways he can call them up, but
they're not new ones. Only you have that ability—
you're still the super-weapon we all seek. And in time
we will have your secret.'

They reached the tank. It was twice the size of any
tank Jake had seen before. It rolled on tracks but had
no barrel and large cylinders were strapped to its side.
Amongst the usual 'danger' and 'biohazard' signs, Jake
could see one he'd first noticed on the Council's island
that denoted 'superpowers'. A ramp extended from the
back of the vehicle. More Enforcers were inside.

'What are you doing about my parents?' asked Jake
as he was pushed up the ramp.

'They are very ill, Hunter. It is unforgivable what you
did to them.'

'I didn't do anything! I was trying to fully restore
their memories. The ones you took!'

'Our doctors are doing the best they can.' A shadow
passed over Kirby's face. 'However, it doesn't seem to
be something we can reverse. If they die, Hunter, it's
your fault.'

Jake struggled, but without powers he could do
nothing against his bonds. An Enforcer rifle-butted him
in the back of the head to calm him down. Jake felt the
world spin, and could feel the blood trickle down the
back of his neck.

'And what about my sister? What are you going to do now you have me?'

'Provided she lives, she is a valuable asset. And if your parents die: an orphan. Then the Foundation will look after her.'

The Enforcers dragged Jake into the tank. His legs buckled from a weakness that suddenly gripped him. He was suffering from the loss of blood and not hooking up to Villain.net.

The access ramp lifted up with a noisy whirl of servos. Jake saw Kirby was watching him like a hawk.

'I'm going to kill you when all this is over,' stated Jake flatly.

He didn't see Kirby's reaction as the door shut. The Enforcers shoved him into a chair, locking a harness around him. Then they took their own seats as a green light started to flash in the dingy interior.

An electronic voice spoke aloud. 'Prepare for jump in three, two, one.'

Jake felt a familiar dizzy feeling that accompanied teleportation.

'Jump complete.'

The rear door suddenly hissed open and a cold wind blasted Jake. The Enforcers unfastened his harness and pushed him outside.

Thick snow fell and the biting cold took Jake's breath away. The tank had teleported onto a hard metal deck.

Captured

He looked around trying to get his bearings. A large steel command tower rose to one side, and to the other—an icy sea.

Jake blinked as his brain processed where he was. He was on the deck of a huge aircraft carrier. A couple of jet fighters were parked at the end of the runway, amongst other teleport tanks and helicopters.

'What is this place?'

'A mobile containment facility,' said an Enforcer pushing him forward. 'Keep walking.'

'They've turned a boat into a prison?'

'No. That.'

The Enforcer pointed starboard. A massive iceberg dwarfed the aircraft carrier. However, this iceberg was far from normal: it had been hollowed out. Towers poked from the crown, manmade windows covered the surface. A large cavernous mouth, on the same level as the aircraft carrier's deck, led inside.

A bridge had been strung between the iceberg and the ship. A figure stood on it, his arms crossed and wearing a smug smile.

'I can't begin to tell you how much I'm looking forward to our reunion.'

Jake felt sick—from both the weakness he was feeling and the fact that the speaker was none other than Chameleon, freed from Jake's castle.

Chameleon slapped Jake hard across the face and

took great satisfaction from seeing Jake collapse. He groaned and didn't rise.

'Miss me?' gloated Chameleon.

A pair of Enforcers each hooked an arm beneath Jake and dragged him across the bridge, into the icy prison.

Jake hoped he had the willpower to stop himself smiling. That would ruin everything.

Lorna once again crept along the corridors of Jake's castle—this time against her own better judgement. Her head was filled with questions that demanded answers. Jake was downloading from Villain.net—she had finally accepted that.

But she needed to know more, needed to know the truth. She couldn't accept Jake was a real villain, especially a member of the Council of Evil. A part of her was convinced it was some gigantic mix up.

When she had released Chameleon they had used his power to teleport back to the Hero Foundation. Chameleon was so dehydrated and in such a physically weak condition that he had been unable to talk. Eric Kirby was delighted to see Chameleon return and had hugged Lorna with a tear in his eye.

Kirby had briefed Lorna on the peril she was in by hanging around with Jake, but he saw the advantage in keeping her close to him. Lorna had been puzzled

Captured

about how much Kirby seemed to know about Jake's operations, but the old man had refused to tell her how he knew so much.

Under Kirby's orders she had returned to the castle to keep an eye on Jake. She had then gone to Baghdad to see for herself how Jake acted. The simple fact that he was facing a third member of the Council of Evil had proved to her that Kirby was confused. There had to be more to Jake than being a supervillain. She had known Jake at school. She knew how he often got into trouble that he didn't cause.

The moment Lorna started seeing the potentially good side of Jake, darker thoughts intruded. How much did Mr Grimm and Munir know about Jake's identity? Did they know he was a villain, or had they been tricked into thinking he was a hero? Or worse still, were they the ones leading him down the wrong path? After all, Munir had killed Igor. Kirby had been surprised to learn Grimm was helping Jake, but had said very little else on the matter to Lorna.

Her thoughts were diverted once again by approaching footsteps. Lorna hid in the shadows of the loft rafters, high above the banqueting hall. Munir had vanished the moment they arrived back at the castle and Lorna had made the most of the time to explore around.

She had found the long-disused banqueting hall on

the upper levels of the castle. Something had caught her eye in the angled roof above. Lorna had flown up into the rafters to get a clearer look. It was a bundle of glowing fibre-optic cables that ran from the wall into the ceiling. They looked freshly laid. She was denied further inspection because Munir entered the hall below.

Munir looked at a satellite videophone in his hand, and then gazed up at the dark ceiling. Lorna shrank back into the shadows, certain that he could see her, but Munir looked back at his phone and spoke in a low voice. The device was obviously more powerful than her mobile phone, able to pick up a signal anywhere in the world.

'I'm right below it. It's on the roof . . . '

Munir dashed back out of the room. Lorna frowned. Below what? Her fingers traced the fibre-optic cable back through a narrow hole in the rooftop. She'd had enough smoke and mirrors, now was the time to get to the bottom of what was going on.

Kirby had made sure she was fully charged with a battery of superpowers for her undercover mission. She mentally selected the power she needed. Lorna touched the rooftop and pushed. Her hand went smoothly through the solid material—and the rest of her body followed.

She was halfway through the roof, and already the

Captured

driving rain had soaked her to the skin. Lightning illuminated the heavens as she pulled her legs through the solid roof. She was now outside and fully exposed to the elements.

Lorna shielded her eyes from the rain, but it wasn't hard to notice the large parabolic dish about ten metres in diameter mounted on a pneumatic gimbal. Massive coils stretched away from the dish and anchored to the four corners of the castle. Lorna could see wires and tubing running down into the stonework. More cables ran from the back, including the fibre optics she had traced from below.

Lightning flashed again, revealing the newness of the construction. Tubes, cables, and wires had been stacked behind a low parapet, shielding them from the wind. The roof prevented the dish from being seen from Jake's Command Centre standing in the far corner of the castle.

Lorna had seen enough diabolical plans to deduce that this was some sort of super-weapon. What was Jake up to?

An access hatch opened across the rooftop. The wind took the thick wooden door and made it slam loudly. Munir climbed from the trapdoor and braced himself against the blustery rain. He carefully walked around the giant device, his eyes wide.

Lorna hid in the shadows. Munir crawled under the

machine and began to unscrew a small service panel. He began attaching the wires inside. It was easy for Lorna to put the pieces together. Munir had been exposing the electrical panels in the room and was now fixing the dish. He was obviously in on the operation. She had to find a way to stop him.

Lightning flashed again. Luckily, Munir was too busy with his task to notice Lorna disappearing through the solid rooftop.

Mr Grimm quick-walked down the Council of Evil's corridors. Sirens were ringing and the corridors were full of guards and supers running to wherever the action was. An automated male voice kept repeating the words:

'Alert! Prisoner escape!'

Grimm didn't have any idea what that was about, but he didn't care. The Council was a nest of vipers, filled with evil plans and double-crossing backstabbers. This would be the last time he walked through these corridors of power. He had been part of many insidious plans over the decades. The last being Chromosome's unsuccessful takeover of the Council. He had known that Jake's venture would yield pretty much the same results, but he had got rid of several of the fools and he had to encourage the boy to try—just in case he was

Captured

successful. The downfall of Amy, Professor Mobius, and Armageddon in quick succession had caused ripples of fear through the Council.

Change was on its way.

Mr Grimm intended to be at the spearhead of that wave of change. He was tired of working for balance on both sides, so had embarked on an extremely ambitious plan. A plan that hinged around Jake Hunter.

And now the boy had gone missing.

Grimm crossed the covered bridge that connected the central island to Momentum's chambers. The doors opened, revealing a bare chamber beyond. Momentum was stuffing his possessions into packing boxes.

'What is going on?' demanded Grimm.

'A high-level prisoner breakout on the island! Necros had some plan that's gone terribly wrong.'

'Why doesn't that surprise me?'

'I don't think you understand, Grimm. The whole world is at crisis point! Lord Eon is almost in power, and he's a villain far worse than any of us!'

'You cannot run from a villain who manipulates time, so why try? If it's the end, so be it. In the meantime we must press ahead as scheduled.'

'That is something I plan to do very far from here!'

Mr Grimm studied the heavily built Momentum. He wondered how long it would be before the villain double-crossed him? It was inevitable, so inevitable that Grimm had already factored into his plan exactly how he would abandon Momentum, using him as a scapegoat. The trick to survival was to be proactive rather than reactive.

'Have you heard from Hunter?' asked Grimm quietly. He was suddenly aware that the intruder alarm had been silenced.

'No. Not since he killed Armageddon.'

Grimm detected a note of fear in Momentum's voice. The implication was obvious—if Hunter could take down somebody as menacing as Armageddon, then Momentum had little hope of survival if Jake turned on him.

'Then Hunter is missing. The last report I received was that he walked into a Foundation Hospital carrying his injured sister.'

'He gave himself up?'

'I doubt that. However, he is now in the hands of the enemy which means all our good work could be for nothing.'

Momentum was thinking fast. There was a glint of panic in his eyes. 'Perhaps we should cut our losses?'

Grimm sneered. 'You are truly a coward. I'm not going to let the Foundation pull Hunter apart, not now we are so close to victory. We must conclude our plan and use Hunter for what he is—the ultimate

Captured

weapon to destroy both the Foundation and the Council! We will return to the castle and prepare the weapon.'

The low temperature helped Jake to keep calm. He had been led through a network of corridors honeycombing the iceberg. Despite the ice-covered walls, the temperature was quite comfortable. Jake thought it must be similar to being inside an igloo, albeit one created on a gigantic scale.

He had been shoved into a circular interrogation chamber, handcuffed to a chair, a steel desk in front of him. He'd endured many an interrogation from Chameleon when he was held at Diablo Island so knew what to expect.

This one would be different.

Minutes passed before Chameleon entered the chamber. He placed a laptop on the table and stared at Jake. He was looking smug, if a little paler than usual. He leaned so close to Jake that he could smell the cheese Chameleon had eaten for lunch.

'Let me make one thing clear, Hunter. Diablo Island was a holiday camp compared to what you're about to go through.'

'How did you get out?'

Chameleon struck Jake across the face, breaking his

nose. Blood trickled onto his lips. Chameleon was crimson with anger.

'You mean from that crystal prison you sealed me in?'

'I saved you from Chromosome,' said Jake flatly. It was true, even if it was an accident.

'I was conscious throughout my captivity. My eyes open to see your ugly face every single day! I could think but not move! You have no idea what it is like to have an itch that you cannot scratch for months. Your thoughts turn dark and you start wishing for it all to end.' Chameleon slapped Jake again. His incarceration had definitely darkened his temperament.

'I thought heroes didn't beat up prisoners?' said Jake, spitting blood from his split lip.

'You're thinking of saints, not heroes. We do whatever we have to, to get the job done. And to answer your question, I was freed by one of your friends. Somebody you trusted who was all too happy to betray you.'

'Igor was only hired help,' said Jake dismissively.

'Your butler? No, it wasn't him.'

Jake felt his stomach churn. He was sure Igor was the mole. If it wasn't him . . . then the list of traitors was short and the answer would not be pleasant. His suspicions fell on Lorna, but he quickly dampened those. His feelings for her were mixed at best.

Captured

'And I'm not going to tell you who. It's better to let you suffer.'

'I will get out, Chameleon. I need to help my parents. Then I'll give myself up willingly.'

Chameleon gave a wide grin. 'How noble of you. I bet that's the first heroic act of your life?'

'I need to help them. I don't have much time.'

'You're right. You don't have time. In fact, for you, time has run out completely. You won't be seeing them again.'

Jake glared at Chameleon. The hero smiled back.

'You'd like to kill me right now, wouldn't you?'

'Yes.'

'But you can't.' Chameleon tapped the light on Jake's snag-net. 'Because of that. Now you're just a boy. A regular, feeble boy.'

Chameleon sat down and opened the laptop. He hooked sensors into a USB port, then jabbed the sharp end into Jake's wrist.

'Ow!'

'The pain will get worse, trust me.'

'What are you doing?'

'Taking samples of your powers and uploading them to the Foundation server to see if there is any difference between your powers now and from the last time.' Chameleon smiled pleasantly. 'With any luck we'll find out your powers are eating you from the inside and you'll die an agonizing death soon. Like your parents.'

Jake closed his eyes and remained silent. Chameleon was surprised. That kind of taunting had always provoked a violent reaction from Jake in the past. Jake looked as if he had suddenly fallen asleep.

Chameleon turned his attention back to the screen. Progress bars showed the status of the sample extraction. It was already on sixty per cent and rising.

Then the bar stopped.

Chameleon blinked and rolled the cursor across the screen to check the computer hadn't crashed. Then the progress bar began to reverse. In a second it was already back down to forty per cent.

'What's happened?' Chameleon mumbled to himself. The computer screen glitched.

'What's the matter?'

Chameleon's head snapped up. Jake was looking at him with a smile.

'Nothing for you to get smug about. It's a computer problem.'

'Like a virus.'

Chameleon opened his mouth to respond—and then realized it wasn't a question. He looked back at Jake with sudden suspicion.

'What have you done?' Chameleon shook his head

Captured

and composed himself. 'You couldn't have done anything because of the snag-net.'

Then he noticed Jake's broken nose and split lip had healed. Chameleon's expression sagged as Jake grinned like a shark.

The handcuffs on Jake's wrist started to glow cherry-red. The metal melted, oozing from his wrist and landing on the ice in a cloud of steam.

'That's impossible,' gasped Chameleon.

Jake was feeling smug. Adil had told him to plan one step ahead of the enemy, and Jake had. Beth's injury had provided just the opportunity he needed.

'When Kirby was gloating over my capture, he told me that the EMP pulse in Baghdad did something to the nanobots inside me that affected my powers. I can't teleport any more, and maybe I've lost a few others too, but my powers . . . they feel different. Slightly scrambled . . . slightly enhanced.' Jake took off the snag-net belt and dropped it on the table. 'It turns out that one of the advantages is that the old snag-belt trick doesn't work on me any more.'

Jake stood up. Chameleon was too flabbergasted to move. 'When you hooked me up to your mainframe I was able to digitally download myself into the system, or part of me anyway. Zooming around your Foundation network, I had access to a lot of interesting stuff. I got *everything* I needed.' Although Jake could have accessed any of the Foundation's files if he had time, he'd been too focused on his mission to bother. Although he had found time to leave a 'package' in the Foundation's security network—something that would help him access the hospital his parents were being treated at. But he wasn't about to reveal that to Chameleon.

'You *wanted* to be plugged into our network?'

'Why do you think I *let* you capture me? Armageddon's father was one of Kirby's founding members. You lot hid him away from his son and I needed to know where. I took Armageddon out, and read his mind. He didn't know where you put him either. But he suspected the location would be indicated somewhere on your computer system. I just had to think of a way to get to it. What easier way than handing myself over to you lot? You're all predictable. I knew you couldn't resist hacking into my powers.'

'Jake . . . I . . . '

Jake moved incredibly fast. He smacked Chameleon's head against the metal table so hard that his face dented the metal. Chameleon groaned from the pain and sagged to the floor; a fireball formed in the hero's palm.

'I don't think so,' snarled Jake.

He looped the snag-belt around Chameleon's neck, pulling it so hard it choked the hero. The fireball

Captured

immediately extinguished as his powers were neutral-ized.

Chameleon tried to crawl away. Jake grabbed his foot and yanked him back.

'You're not going anywhere, mate. I think I should flex these new powers a little to see exactly what I'm capable of.'

The Enforcers who had transported Jake were stowing the tele-tank at the end of the aircraft carrier. Once it was secured, their shift was over and they could finally go and eat.

A loud cracking sound got their attention. As one, they turned to the iceberg. Huge fissures appeared along the top, making thunder-like sounds.

Then the entire peak of the iceberg exploded. Its surface area was twenty times bigger than the aircraft carrier. Huge chunks of ice, some the size of stately homes, flew in every direction. A massive block of ice spun towards the defenceless Enforcers—

It raked across the deck centimetres from them. One Enforcer still had his hand on the tele-tank as the ice swept the vehicle—and a dozen jet fighters—over the edge and into the icy water. Another piece of ice hur-tled through the sky like a meteor, smashing the bridge apart.

Chunks of ice rained down, forcing everybody on deck to cover their faces. Some of the Enforcers noticed a figure shoot skyward from the iceberg like a rocket. They had no time to identify the super before the larger chunks of ice fell into the ocean—kicking up enormous tidal waves that reached as high as the carrier's deck.

They fled for cover, praying they would not be washed overboard.

Jake didn't even bother looking down as he punctured through the heavy clouds so fast that he created a sonic boom. He was whooping with delight—his plan to find Leech had worked, and his powers flowed through his body like fire. He wondered if Chameleon had been crushed under all the ice, but even that didn't bother him too much.

He'd soon have Leech's power to be able to steal both the poison cure and Psych's powers from Pete.

Right now, he felt indestructible.

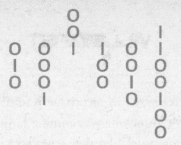

The Traitor's Path

The landscape was bleak, comprising browns, greys, and snow-capped mountains of the Himalayas. Jake looked around hoping for a sign he was in the right place. At these great altitudes the air was so thin that Jake was feeling light-headed. Then he heard a faint clacking noise above the ever-present wind.

Jake glided through the air, following the noise. He landed near a circular cylinder that spun in the wind. It was a Buddhist prayer wheel covered with carvings. Further along the plateau, lines of brightly coloured flags fluttered in the breeze. They all led towards a magnificent Buddhist temple built on the peak of the mountain. A long, winding stairway was the only approach—if you didn't possess superpowers.

Jake flew to the entrance. The gates were huge, inlaid with gold and probably worth a small fortune. Jake raised his hand to knock but the gate opened up before he could.

A young bald monk greeted him. 'He is expecting you.'

'He is?' asked Jake in surprise. Up until ten minutes ago he hadn't known he was coming himself. Jake had discovered computer files that revealed Kirby had hidden Leech in a Buddhist temple in the Himalayas.

Inside the temple it was overly warm and dark, lit only by streamers of light falling through high windows. Lanterns were hung around a great hall that was decorated with long, colourful swatches of cotton. The air smelt sweet and heavy. It was the most relaxing place he had ever been to and Jake had to battle to keep his eyelids open.

The monk led Jake to an old man, about Eric Kirby's age, who sat on a cushion. The monk bowed and left.

Bemused, Jake watched as the monk closed the hall door, leaving them alone. The old man hadn't moved. His eyes were closed. Jake started to get a sinking feeling.

'I hope you're not dead.'

'So do I,' came the sharp voice from the old man. 'Sit.'

Jake sighed and reluctantly sat opposite. 'Are you Leech?'

The old man opened his eyes and studied Jake. There was a mischievous twinkle in them. Finally, he responded.

'I have been known by that name.'

'Look, I don't mean to be rude, but I need your help.

The Traitor's Path

I need your power so I can extract an antidote from an enemy to save my parents.'

'My power? And what makes you think I still have it? Life is like the seasons. Autumn years wither away the salad days of your life . . . until old age greets you.'

Jake felt a wave of despair. 'You don't have your powers any more? I know they fade with age, but some of you keep them. Like Eric Kirby. He was your friend, he still possesses his.'

'Ah, yes. Dear Eric Kirby. I'm sure he is well. He was the one who placed me here, out of harm's reach from my son. You know him? You know of Armageddon?'

'I know he is your son.' Jake thought it wise not to mention that a bomb had eliminated the villain.

The old man looked deep into Jake's eyes. 'You are a troubled boy. Plagued by constant ill fortune. Bad luck seems to dog your heels. Everything you do, everything you touch, fails or crumbles.'

The words stung Jake. It was one thing to think that himself, but quite another to hear it from a stranger. Then he suddenly stood up and looked around the hall, alert. He didn't sense danger, but the monk had been expecting him and the old man seemed to know a lot about him—it was better that he was on his guard.

'You jump at your own shadow, boy.'

Jake looked nervously around. 'Have I walked into a trap?'

'Not yet. You are safe here. Sit.'

Jake warily sat back down. 'What do you mean "not yet"?'

The old man ignored the question. 'I have learnt much during my time here. I'm a Prime, full of amazing power and potential. And yet here, in the middle of nowhere, I discover things that continue to amaze me.'

Jake was growing impatient. 'That's really interesting. Look, my parents are dying and I—'

'So am I.'

Jake shut up. He didn't know how to react to that candid statement.

'Very soon. In fact, I have been waiting for you to arrive, Jake Hunter.'

Jake eyed the entrance to the hall again; his hackles rose.

'How do you know about me?'

'Old Kirby placed me here, in this remote place, for my safety. He was so concerned that he ensured I could not leave.'

Jake frowned. The old man's tone sounded spiteful. 'This is a prison?'

'This is a paradise . . . that so happens to be a prison.'

Jake inhaled, ready to ask another question, but the old man answered it before he could speak. 'He saw me as a threat. One who can absorb and take a couple of powers from another is a threat indeed. I can only retain them for a short time, enough to use them or allow the Foundation to extract them from me for their website.'

'That's how they got so many powers?'

'Thanks to me, yes. The ones that were not donated willingly were . . . taken.'

'But if you helped Kirby set up the Foundation then why didn't he trust you not to use your powers on him?'

'Oh he did, for a short while. But I betrayed that trust. I leeched one of his powers. I intended only that it went onto Hero.com, but Kirby took exception and grew angry. He couldn't kill an old friend, could he? But placing him in this rather elaborate nursing home did the same trick as killing me. Here . . . away from my son. Away from the Foundation.'

'Look, I'm sure this history is fascinating on any other day. But my parents are dying. Are you going to help?'

'Jake Hunter, you are walking into a world of betrayal and connivance.'

'You can see the future?'

'No, only the present. I know that doesn't sound terribly impressive, but it is the gift of second sight. The same one I took from Kirby.'

'I thought you said the powers wore off you?'

The old man smiled mischievously. 'Well, this one stuck. With my second sight I can see the trouble that is brewing around you. You are in great danger. Many see you as the ultimate weapon.'

'I know that.'

'Then you should know that forces are at work to entrap you. You don't have much time before friends become enemies.'

'I don't have any friends.'

'Oh, you do. And now you have another. Me. I willingly offer my power to you.'

Leech held out his wrist. Jake was so surprised by the sudden philanthropic display that he momentarily forgot about the sonic-extractor in his jacket. He positioned it over the man's wrist and activated the device. The glass vial filled with a sparkling yellow substance. Jake stared at it.

'This is it?'

'Yes.' Jake positioned the sonic-extractor over his own wrist. If he hit the button the device would inject the power into him.

'Be warned, once you use it on yourself then you have only minutes in which to use it before the effects start to wear off. Save it for the right time.' Jake nodded and put the gadget back into his jacket.

The old man leant forward, extending a finger to nudge the glass pendant around Jake's neck. It was the one he had snagged from Armageddon and hadn't had time to put with the others.

'Where did you get this?'

'I . . . I got it from a Council Member.'

'One you have killed. They wouldn't give such a treasure up freely. My son wears one.'

'What is it?'

'One of six keys to obtain a Core Power. You know what they are?'

'Yes. You were supposed to try and obtain one.'

'Try? I did it. It was a wondrous power . . . and a deadly one.'

'So what happened to it?'

'We realized that it was too powerful to try and replicate, and too dangerous to store. No one side should possess such a power.'

Jake's eyes gleamed. 'What was the power?'

The old man studied him carefully. 'The power was so potent it was split into six components, and those were placed in the pendants, one of which you have.'

Jake held the pendant up to the soft light. It was perfectly transparent.

'The six pendants were distributed between the leaders of the Council and the Foundation with the notion that neither side would ever have them all. Necros has one, Kirby the other. I know some of the

Council have killed key members of the Foundation and obtained their pendants.'

'And if somebody got all six . . . they would have one of the Core Powers?'

'Yes, and in the wrong hands the world could end and the fabric of the universe be torn asunder, such is their strength.'

Jake's mouth went dry. He thought it best not to mention that he already had half the pendants.

'Keep it safe. Now you owe me a favour.'

Jake hesitated. He was ready to jump back to his castle so he could locate Pete and extract the antidote, but the old man had been kind enough to him so he paused to listen.

'My body may have been trapped here, but my mind has not. In all those years I have harboured a grudge against Kirby for what he did to me. In this temple I have the Foundation's secrets, including Kirby's most guarded ones. When your task is over I ask only that you return and carry out my wishes.' He tapped an ornate box sitting to one side. 'You may open it on your return.'

Jake felt a wave of sympathy for the ex-hero. He nodded.

'I promise.'

The old man didn't reply. He had closed his eyes again, deep in meditation or possibly dead. Jake didn't want to find out which. He crossed the chamber and closed his own eyes and opened a quantum tunnel to his castle. His eyes were fixed on the old man as he walked through.

Something was wrong. Jake sensed it the moment the portal closed behind him. He checked a few rooms on the lower level but found nothing amiss. Then he heard the faintest of sounds from above: it sounded like sobbing. Lorna? He felt a rush of relief that she was still alive after Baghdad. So much had happened that he had relied on Munir to take her back to the safety of the castle.

Jake silently ascended to the upper levels. The sobbing was coming from the banqueting hall ahead.

'Lorna?'

He opened the door and walked into the room. Lorna wasn't there and the room had been trashed. The floor and wall panels had been torn away revealing metal panels that pulsed with energy. They were etched with fine lines like some giant circuit board. The lines spiralled around the room, all centring on one point in the ceiling.

Jake was completely baffled. Before he could react, sections of the floor rose around him, fluidly transforming in three dimensions. Billions of metal particles flowed like treacle, forming metal braces around his feet and raising him in the air. Metal work from above clanked as it morphed, snatching his hands and pulling him into an x-position. Metal spheres encased around his hands and he yelled with fury—it was a trap.

Jake fired a radioactive streamer—the spherical manacles glowed brilliantly but absorbed the energy. Across from him, Jake could just see a dozen glass cylinders, the size of a man, appearing from behind a metal shield. Liquid powers started to fill the cylinders. The flow only stopped when he ceased his attack.

'Keep going!' said a familiar voice from behind him.

Jake's shackles twisted him round so he could face: Momentum. The big man laughed heartily. The room had transformed around them. It now resembled the insides of some giant machine. It was completely unrecognizable.

'The angrier you become the happier we'll be.'

Jake screamed and felt his vision tingeing red as rage overtook him. Momentum now appeared as a series of electrical pulses as his vision highlighted the villain's nervous system. The last time Jake had been this angry the results had been terrible and he had mutated his best friend beyond recognition.

The Traitor's Path

More raw power filled the cylinders as Jake launched another attack at the manacles. The assault had no effect on the metal. Momentum laughed.

'It's tyrillium! You know you can't destroy that.'

'What do you want?' screamed Jake.

'You. Isn't it obvious? You are the super-weapon both sides have longed to possess. And now you're mine.'

'The Council will pay for this!'

'The Council knows nothing about this. I stand for a third party. Necros asked you to investigate Forge, and you did nothing about it because you were so wrapped up in your own little power play. I helped create Forge. It is the new rising power, and you have fulfilled your destiny and become our super-weapon! This entire castle has been modified as a weapon that harnesses your powers.'

'But Forge was in Venice . . . stopping our plans!'

'But you didn't see them attack me, did you? They went after you as a decoy so that you wouldn't suspect my involvement with them.'

Jake struggled futilely against his restraints. He was feeling a fool for being misled so much. Then he stopped as something occurred to him.

'How did you find my base?'

'Find it? It was my idea to put you here. Maybe you should meet my co-conspirator? Enter!'

The door opened and Mr Grimm came in. Jake was speechless. Of all the people he never would have suspected of betraying him—the one who had helped him the most.

'Grimm? Why?'

'There is only so much you can achieve in maintaining a balance between good and evil, so Momentum and I created the neutral component and called it Forge. A group made from both heroes and villains, all focused on the desire for neutrality. When Basilisk created you, he created a weapon everybody needed. A weapon powered by your rage. Of course, you would not willingly walk into the heart of such a device . . . unless you thought it was somewhere you were safe. We put you here and constructed the weapon around you.'

Momentum tapped a button on the console. A holographic display floated in the air. 'It took us longer than we planned. We had hoped that Chromosome would have built you into such a rage that we could harness your unique powers. But that was not enough. We needed more. You needed to be angrier to unleash those powers.'

Grimm continued. 'So that's when it occurred to me to use your sister.'

'You? It's your fault she's fighting me?'

Energy crackled across Jake's body. He was beyond

anger and now had no control over it. Away from the machine the energy blast would have destroyed the room, but instead it was channelled into the construct and the power was stored in the cylinders.

Momentum's eyes were wide as his computer analysed the deposit. 'That was a good one! A previously undiscovered power! Good, good!'

'You see, that is exactly why Beth was such a useful asset. Being a double agent I could easily convince Kirby to use the girl as a pawn. There was no way we could make her as powerful as you, but I wagered even somebody as morally bankrupt as yourself would not willingly harm his own sister. Which made her the perfect tool.'

Jake writhed and spat—energy roared from his body, only to be caught and turned into its component forms and stored in the rapidly filling cylinders.

Momentum laughed, he was enjoying taunting Jake. For too long he had been forced to act pleasantly to the little upstart. 'And making you poison your parents was a delicious idea, guaranteed to drive you crazy.'

Jake barely heard the words. His body shuddered violently as multiple powers unleashed—all absorbed by the machine. From the outside, the entire castle seemed to glow. Electronic panels were embedded into almost every wall, designed to soak in and break down the fierce onslaught Jake was producing.

Momentum continued, 'Of course, Pete messed things up. Your parents should have died instantly. I suppose the boy doesn't quite possess that killer instinct yet. But rest assured, they are slowly dying, and there is nothing you can do about it.'

Grimm paced around Jake. 'By taking out Armageddon, you have helped our cause. It has all been a carefully crafted plan from the very beginning. I knew you would never suspect me; you are so trusting. This current problem with Lord Eon delayed us again. Momentum had to assist the Council in stopping that problem, which put us back by several days. But here you are. Here we are, ready to drop our allegiances to the Foundation and the Council—ready to launch the most powerful of all forces. All thanks to you.'

'You better pray I don't escape from here—or you'll both be dead!'

'Idle threats, boy. Idle threats. Now, to see the extent of our weapon we have pre-programmed two targets to eliminate.'

The holographic screen split into two, displaying a satellite image of a complex building on one side and a small island on the other that was bristling with communication towers.

Mr Grimm pointed to the images. 'On the right we have the Council's main communication relay stations. By taking that out we will hinder Villain.net.

Only for a couple of hours, but enough to make our point. On the left is a Foundation hospital.' He stared levelly at Jake. 'The very one your parents and sister are in.'

'No!'

'Commence firing procedure!' commanded Mr Grimm.

Momentum ran a diagnostic through the computer. 'Target locked and the system is fully charged.'

'Fire.'

The entire room glowed with a kaleidoscope of colour. Almost every room in the castle illuminated as the panels within them surged with energy. The liquid powers in two of the cylinders were shot into the system under high pressure.

The parabolic dish on the castle roof shot a brilliant beam of light into the sky that lasted for three seconds before fading.

Everybody watched the holographic screen in anticipation. Moments later the stream of energy appeared above the Council island and blasted the complex in a supernova of energy that obscured the destruction. When the light faded away, all that remained of the island was a series of rocks that the sea rushed in to claim.

'Total annihilation!' declared Momentum.

'Excellent! Target the hospital.'

Momentum recalibrated the machine. Jake shouted, angrier than he had ever been—which only served to replace the liquid powers.

'No! Don't do this! Stop!'

'Target locked,' said Momentum with a grin.

Mr Grimm didn't hesitate. 'Fire.'

Once again the room glowed—then the entire castle shook. A massive explosion resonated across the building.

Anybody watching outside would have seen the west wing of the castle explode in a shower of rubble, wild energy streamers forking out at the landscape beyond.

Grimm and Momentum looked around in shock as the systems wound down.

'What happened?' demanded Grimm.

Momentum consulted the computer. 'A power surge. It looks like the dampers in the west wing have exploded.'

'That's impossible . . . unless . . . they've been sabotaged.'

Munir dropped down from the rafters, poised to strike.

'Well deduced. I've been sabotaging this weapon from the moment I found out about it.'

Hope flickered through Jake. 'Munir!! Get me out of this thing!'

The Traitor's Path

'Shut up!' snarled Munir. 'You're no better than these two scumbags!'

Jake was confused and struggled at his bonds. What was going on?

'What are you doing, Munir? I gave you back your powers. I trusted you.'

'Then you're the fool, Hunter!' Jake sagged—it was now clear Munir had told Kirby they were in Baghdad, and that's how Beth had found him.

Munir continued. 'After you approached me in Istanbul wanting to know how to locate the Hooded Harrier, I did feel sorry for you. But then I realized that I had the perfect bargaining chip to go to Eric Kirby and get my powers back via Hero.com. I contacted him through Hero.com when I was back in Turkey. He refused, not knowing what the risks would be hooking a Prime to the website. He was also aware of a double agent within the Foundation ranks. Him.' He pointed a finger at Grimm. 'So my job was to befriend you and work out a way to bring you to the Foundation. When I discovered Grimm's double-dealings ran deep in the Foundation I was forced to stay by your side longer than planned. Then I discovered what had happened to Chameleon. You had imprisoned him here.'

Munir stared banefully at Jake. 'However, Lorna freed him before I could. I wish I could have told her everything, but I had to be deep undercover and couldn't risk it. I returned here and searched the castle further. That's when I discovered that Grimm had formed Forge and was using this place as a giant weapon. I have been sabotaging the weapon every time I was here. You should thank me for that.'

Jake said nothing. His red vision returned to normal as he fought to control his temper. If Grimm and Momentum wanted him to use it, then he wouldn't give them the pleasure.

'Enough of this nonsense!' shouted Grimm. 'Take the hero!'

Momentum pawed his foot on the ground like a bull and charged forward with a surprising turn of speed.

Munir formed an ice wall and slid aside. Momentum crashed through the ice and abruptly stopped—spinning to face Munir again.

'Come 'ere!' Momentum snarled and smashed his fist into his palm. A boom echoed around the room and a crack appeared in the floor, racing towards Munir. As the floorboards ripped away, parts of the metal floor fell into the room below.

'Stop!' yelled Grimm. 'You're destroying the weapon!'

Momentum growled and thundered towards Munir as the hero leapt aside. Momentum changed his angle of attack to follow him.

The Traitor's Path

Munir had been hoping for that. He shot black ice onto the floor.

Momentum hit the ice and flailed wildly out of control. He had increased his speed and mass and now there was no way he could stop. Munir's moment of triumph was cut short as the bulky villain cannoned into him.

The thick castle wall smashed away. The tyrillium metal held, but the ancient brickwork behind it didn't. Metal panels detached as both Momentum and Munir plummeted down the vertical cliff that surrounded three sides of the castle. Wind and rain drove into the gaping hole, blanketing the men's yells.

Grimm ran over to the hole in the wall and peered out. He guessed Munir must still be alive because the rain immediately turned into hailstones. Golf ball sized balls of ice clipped Grimm on the head and pounded the valley below.

Jake used the distraction to work his arm in the clamp. The metal might be almost indestructible, but the damaged floor and walls had created gaps in the panels and given the entire construction free-play. When Jake moved his arms and legs, his bindings shifted. If he could just lever his limbs out . . .

'Nice try, Hunter.' Grimm had turned his attention back to Jake. 'Those fools may fight, but I still have you captive. Victory will not be taken from me!'

A fireball suddenly struck Mr Grimm in the chest. The villain skidded across the room, crumpling in a corner. Jake blinked in surprise—his mouth hung open in astonishment.

Lorna had phased through the roof and stood on the rafters, flames still tickling the palms of her hands. Her expression was fierce and for a second Jake thought he would be her next target. To his surprise she flew over to his arm braces and lightly touched them. The metal turned into fine grains and trickled to the floor, releasing him. She did the same for his feet, the almost indestructible metal turning into fine sand. The rest of the panels around the room dissolved in rapid succession. The cylinders shattered, oozing raw power over the floor. In seconds, Grimm's über-machine was nothing more than a pile of silver dust.

'How . . . ?' said Jake, utterly impressed.

'You should try reading sometimes. Tyrillium is a nanobot material, made from billions of microscopic machines. I downloaded the power to deactivate them.'

'Lorn . . . you're my hero,' laughed Jake.

Lorna stared angrily at him. 'You're using Villain.net.'

'Yes. Not by choice. You saw me take out those Council heads.'

Lorna stared at him for a long moment. Jake couldn't read her expression. Her fists were balled, an unmistakable sign she was ready to attack. He braced himself.

The Traitor's Path

Instead Lorna whirled round and blasted Grimm again as he tried to stand. She advanced on him.

'We trusted you! You traitor!'

Grimm gasped between breaths. 'Lorna . . . understand. It was for the greater good. Have mercy! I did all this to maintain pure neutrality. I—'

'You betrayed everybody who looked to you for help. You don't deserve my mercy.'

'He's mine!' yelled Jake and flew over to the cowering Grimm.

'I told you to trust nobody, Hunter. You should have listened. But perhaps we now understand one another and we can work together?'

Jake dragged Grimm over to the oozing raw superpowers that the villains had extracted from his system.

'This is what you wanted, Grimm. This is what burns through my veins and makes my life miserable. Well, you can have it.'

He shoved Grimm's face into the colourful sticky liquid. Grimm screamed as the powers burned his face like acid. He thrashed out, but Jake's grip was too strong. Grimm's face transformed into a hideous skull—his natural state when using his own powers. Still the gloop hissed at his face, stripping and dissolving skin and bone.

Lorna looked away—it was a gruesome way to go.

Jake was unrelenting; merciless. His eyes flared red like a demon as he forced Grimm's head back into the powers. Mr Grimm gurgled and thrashed, but he was no match for Jake's grip.

Finally, the screams subsided and all that remained of Mr Grimm was a shapeless designer suit that soon dissolved in the pool of superpowers. Not a scrap of organic material remained.

Jake breathed hard, forcing himself to cool down before he faced Lorna. She appeared pale and frightened as she looked from the remains of Grimm to Jake.

'He would have tried to kill us both,' stated Jake flatly.

Lorna nodded.

Jake glanced through the hole in the castle wall. The hailstorm was increasing in intensity.

'I think Munir and Momentum are still slugging it out. I have no intention of hanging around to save either of them. I have to hunt down your friend, Pete. He tried to poison my parents and he has the cure inside him. The question is: what are you going to do? You're the hero.'

Lorna stared at Jake for a long moment. Her emotions were in turmoil. She had got close to Jake and really liked him—but to find out what he really was . . .

'You're a villain, Jake. Whichever way you look at it.'

The Traitor's Path

She shook her head. The world was changing around her at a rapid pace. Pete was supposed to be a hero too, but he had turned into something unrecognizable. Maybe there was hope for Jake too?

She had to decide quickly.

Then the entire wall was suddenly blown apart in a massive energy blast. Bricks bounced off both Jake and Lorna.

When Jake looked up his heart sank—Beth was hovering in the gap, ribbons of energy snaking from her fingers, ready to strike.

'Hunter! It's the end of the line for you!'

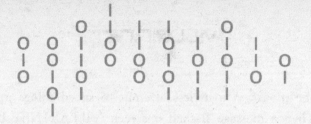

The Last Battle

Jake grabbed Lorna by the wrist and ran for the door. They leapt through as Beth demolished the partitioning wall behind them. It was like a bomb had gone off in the banqueting hall. The wall she destroyed was a load-bearing wall—and half the roof above came down on top of her, including a ton of tyrillium nano-particles.

A huge dust cloud rolled over Jake and Lorna. Jake coughed, pushing bricks off him. Beth was buried beneath them, but he knew it was only a matter of time before she broke through.

Jake examined his options. He needed to get away, but was feeling weak after being hooked up to Grimm's weapon. He charged towards the winding stairs leading to his Command Centre.

'Lorn, come on!'

They made it to the top of the tower. All they could hear was the drumming of hailstones on the windows. Jake darted behind a computer and accessed Villain.net. The connection was slow and he banged the mouse in a useless attempt to speed things up. Then a message flashed onscreen: VILLAIN.NET IS OFFLINE.

'What?' He hit the keyboard in frustration—splintering it in half. Then he remembered Momentum had taken out the Council's main relay station. He would have to make do with what he had inside him.

'We're leaving!' he shouted at Lorna. 'Grab hold of me and don't let go.'

Lorna reached out her hand—but they didn't make contact. Beth chose that moment to fly past and fire at the base of the tower. A fierce stream of energy chewed the brickwork.

'Oh, hell!' shouted Jake as the entire tower shuddered.

The masonry at the base was demolished under Beth's attack. Like a felled tree, the tower slowly toppled towards the main part of the castle. The roof was already missing on the northern side, but the tower came down dead centre.

Inside, the computer equipment pelted Jake and Lorna. Everything jumped in the air and hung there as the tower fell. Despite all their powers there was little either of them could do except ride it out.

The tower broke through the central roof—crumbling down onto the main staircase below. Interior walls folded inwards like a deck of cards as the plush staircase was torn from the walls. The remains of the tower drove through the upper floor, breaking into rubble as it reached the lower floor.

Beth flew over the destruction. A huge pall of dust rose from the rubble. Electrics sparked below, causing fires that were fuelled by the driving wind. A gas main ignited and a brilliant blue fireball punched up, almost knocking Beth from the sky. She could feel the intense heat as she banked aside.

In the debris below, Jake groaned with the effort of maintaining an energy shield around him and Lorna. Tons of rubble hung over their heads and could easily crush them to death with or without healing powers.

'I can't keep this up much longer,' Jake grunted. His body was feeling depleted since Grimm had sucked some of the powers from him and without recharging from V-net it was only a matter of time before he collapsed from fatigue.

He dropped to his knees; the shield around him sagged with his movements. Huge wooden beams and rubble pressed closer. It was becoming very hot in the confined bubble and sweat rolled down his forehead, stinging his eyes.

'Find a way out of this.'

'We could teleport?' said Lorna, looking for any possible escape route. 'I didn't download the power. But if you can . . .'

Jake shook his head. 'My teleportation power has gone and if I open a quantum tunnel this thing will collapse on us both before we can get through. Try that.' He pointed to a half-metre vent in the wall, covered by a metal grid. Lorna blasted the grid with the laser vision she had downloaded. She poked her head into the gap beyond.

'It's a chute going down.'

'I think it's a ventilation shaft for the hangar.'

'You *think*?'

'Lorna! We don't have time. Go through it!'

The debris groaned above their heads. Jake's arms were beginning to shake. Lorna pushed herself in head first. She got as far as her waist before gravity took over and she fell, screaming all the way.

Jake scrabbled on his knees towards the vent. He got both legs through, then dropped down.

The rubble dropped on the empty space they had just vacated. Jake plummeted, trying to control his fall with his flying power.

He was moving fast when he hit the curved bottom and rolled out into the hangar, careering into Lorna.

The hangar was built into the base of the cliff, but they could still hear the dull rumble of the demolished castle above.

'Are you OK?' Jake asked Lorna, helping her stand.

The Last Battle

She nodded, wiping the dust from her dirty clothes. 'Thanks for saving me back there.'

Lorna nodded, eventually finding her words. 'I should really bring you into the Foundation, Jake. As a prisoner.'

'They did that twice already. They stuck needles in me to discover why I'm different.'

'Why are you different?'

'It's a long story involving Basilisk.'

'Basilisk?' Lorna had encountered that villain before.

'I'll tell you another time. But all that the Foundation is after is exactly the same thing Grimm and Momentum wanted. They want to use me as a super-weapon. That's all they want. And they'll keep on coming after me.'

Lorna nodded, deep in thought.

'And that girl. That's your sister? I heard Mr Grimm gloating how they had trained her to fight you.'

'She has no memory of who I am. Neither do my parents. I have to find your friend Pete to extract a cure from him to save their lives and restore their memories. Whatever you choose to do to me, it will have to wait until I achieve that.'

Lorna nodded again. 'In that case I should come with you. Help you.'

The hangar door suddenly buckled.

'I know you're in there, Hunter!'

Jake was startled. 'How did she find us?'

Beth pounded the doors again. She wouldn't dare teleport inside since she didn't know the layout of the hangar and didn't want to materialize sandwiched halfway through something.

Jake arced his finger though the air and opened up a quantum tunnel.

'Let's go.'

They leapt through, the tunnel closing behind them.

Lorna looked around. They were standing on a tiny tropical island that was dominated by a single mansion house. The island was so small they could see the ocean through the open doors on the opposite side of the house.

'Where are we?'

'This is Pete's hideout. I've been here before. It's the only place I can think he'll be.'

Lorna sagged, burning with jealousy. 'This is Pete's? How? I've been moaning for ages that the Foundation doesn't reward us. Pete turns bad and gets a tropical holiday home and you get your own castle. Life's so unfair!'

Jake wasn't listening. He was running from room to room, his desperation mounting.

'He's not here, and with everything in my base destroyed, I don't know how we can find him.'

The Last Battle

A quantum tunnel suddenly ripped open right next to Lorna. Jake expected to see Pete—instead a flurry of hailstones bounced into the tropical mansion and Beth stepped out.

Lorna seized the moment of hesitation. She didn't dare harm Jake's sister with her energy blast. Instead she grabbed the massive plasma TV next to her. Assisted by her enhanced strength, Lorna swung the television over Beth's head. The TV folded over her skull. The impact was enough to drop her to the floor—more out of surprise than pain.

Jake had already opened another quantum tunnel and pulled Lorna through.

They appeared on the small island of St Helena. It was where Jake had first met Chromosome. It was remote and a place Beth had no knowledge of. They would be safe enough to collect their thoughts.

But no sooner had Jake sealed the portal than another one opened. Jake could see Pete's luxury villa beyond—and Beth with her arm extended.

A crackling stream of lightning shot from her fingers, tunnelling from the luxury Caribbean island thousands of miles away to strike Jake in the chest. He was flung down the hillside.

Beth jumped through the portal and was blindsided by Lorna as energy bolts fired from her eyes. Beth spun sideways into a tree, using her only hand to stop her

from falling any further. Lorna flew down the hill and grabbed Jake.

'We have to get out of here!'

Jake opened another portal and they leapt through— this time appearing in Sydney Harbour. Lorna looked around in surprise, noticing the reconstruction efforts taking place on the famous Opera House.

'I've always wanted to come here!' she said with a laugh.

Still Beth followed. Jake opened another portal and ran through. Each portal was dwindling his energy and he knew he didn't have a lot left. He racked his memory to picture all the places he had been before—anywhere that might offer a quick getaway. They appeared outside Lorna's house, on a volcanic island, a housing estate in Scotland—scaring a couple of kids who were kicking a football around. Still, Beth unerringly followed. They finally appeared in the grounds of a university in Istanbul.

'How is she doing this?' demanded Jake.

'She must be tracking us somehow.' Lorna suddenly stared at her wrist. 'My CUCI! She works for the Foundation, she must be tracking my CUCI!'

Then an idea struck Jake. 'That's how I can find Pete!' He remembered that Grimm had removed Pete's CUCI and replaced it with a tracking beacon before he woke from the coma. He'd completely forgotten.

The Last Battle

That's how he found Pete just after he had escaped from the hospital. His hand patted his jacket and he pulled out the slim locator Grimm had given him.

'I know how to find Pete! Come on!'

'I can't. I'm putting you in danger. You'll have to go without me.'

Jake hesitated. Right now he needed support; he was feeling too weak to face Pete alone. The air tore open behind them and Beth forced her way through. The strain of the constant tunnelling was showing on her face.

Lorna pushed Jake away. 'Go! I'll hold her off.'

Jake wanted to say something, thank Lorna for helping him against all odds, but he couldn't find the words. He glanced at the location on the tracker beacon and tunnelled away. The last thing he saw was his sister launching a volley of superpowers at Lorna.

Jake appeared outside a bank. He wasn't sure where he was in the world and the writing on the side of the bank was not immediately recognizable. A glance at his locator confirmed Pete was inside. This was further proved when alarms sounded from within.

Pete was robbing the bank!

'You moron!' muttered Jake under his breath. Pete had phenomenal powers and could do almost anything—instead he chose such a small and unimpressive target.

The doors to the bank burst open and three figures ran out carrying bags of cash. There were two men and a redheaded teenage girl, all wearing the same insignia on their chest. Jake recognized the logo as the one worn by his Forge attackers in Venice. This was more superpowered trouble he didn't need right now.

Pete clomped out of the bank, several feet taller than normal. His skin a sickening cyan colour and cracked all over. He was laughing as the thieves ran across the road to their getaway van—the same vehicle Jake was hiding behind.

Jake took the sonic-extractor from his pocket and pressed it against his arm. Leech's power transferred into his system. Jake felt the slight tingle and the boost of energy he received from taking the power. He took a deep breath and stepped out.

'Pete!'

Pete stopped in his tracks, evidently surprised to see Jake.

'Hunter? What are you doing here?'

Jake snarled and held out his hand, flashing the Draizor. It seemed like months had passed since he had bought it from Momentum—but in reality it had only been days. This was exactly the situation he needed it for.

He activated the Draizor. A piercing data whine

played loudly. Pete shrieked in pain, clutching his ears as he dropped to his knees.

One of the Forge men transformed his hands into large, calloused, mallets that could shatter a skull with a single blow. Jake blew the man on his back with a single black fireball. He was surprised to find the EMP was still affecting his powers. He was curious how long those effects would last.

The second man hesitated—but the girl snorted flames from her mouth. Smoke curled from her nostrils and her hair burst into flame, but she didn't seem to notice.

'Not today, little girl!' growled Jake. He pointed at her—and the girl instantly froze on the spot, paralysed. The third Forge agent wisely decided to teleport away.

Pete convulsed in pain; his bulky body shrank back to normal size. Jake stopped the Draizor.

'You're going to give me that power now, mate.'

Pete's voice was feeble. 'Get lost . . . '

Jake thumbed the Draizor again. The sharp sounds sent agony through Pete's head. Blood started to trickle from his ears. Jake silenced the machine.

'This time I don't have to be nice and ask. You almost killed my parents, Pete.'

Pete looked frightened. 'I didn't mean to.'

'I know Momentum made you do it. But after the kindness I showed you . . . '

'Kindness? You were only kind because you wanted something from me.'

'That doesn't matter any more. I'm going to drag it out of you. I hope this really hurts.'

Jake summoned Leech's power. It was the mental equivalent of sorting through old drawers and cupboards. Jake simply knew what powers Pete possessed and how to draw them out. He immediately targeted the poison Pete had created. By the time Jake had extracted it he could see how to reverse the process to make the cure. Next, he took the remnants of Psych's memory restoration power. This was the golden grail Jake had been pursuing—the one power that would restore his parents' memories.

Leech had told him that he was limited to the number of powers he could extract at any one time and that they only lasted for a limited amount of time.

During his long brooding over how he would get revenge on Pete for trying to assassinate his family, he had triggered and created a suite of superpowers that bubbled through his system. They were all malicious, all deadly. He recalled Adil's words over the chess game—strategy and patience led to victory.

Jake inserted one of his creations into Pete and broke the connection. He studied Pete's face. He was none the wiser. Jake smiled to himself, but it was a mirthless smile. Jake could trigger the smart-virus he had inserted into Pete at any time. Once everything was over, he would let Pete know and watch with great satisfaction as the boy begged for his life.

Jake kicked the cowering boy over.

'You better hope our paths don't cross again, mate.'

Jake didn't have time to punish Pete the way he wanted—he would leave that pleasure for another time.

His parents needed the poison antidote as quickly as possible.

Jake's energy had been bolstered a little by taking Pete's powers, but he still wasn't operating at peak performance and he still had to get through the hospital's security to reach his parents.

During the brief time he had accessed Chameleon's laptop, he had taken the liberty of looking at the hospital layout and locating the exact private ward his parents were in. He'd even had a fleeting glance at a live feed from a security camera in the quad outside, so he could now appear close to the ward entrance.

The online database also detailed the exact position of security. Fifty Enforcers patrolled the grounds. The lobby and corridors were swarming with Enforcers and a pair of teenage Downloaders guarded the door to the room. Kirby had anticipated Jake's arrival and he guessed, after the destruction of the Foundation's ice prison, that they were prepared to use absolute force to capture him.

This was the final assault. It was now or never. He was weak but summoned every ounce of power he had.

Jake's portal opened in the quad. It was night, which suited Jake perfectly. Five Enforcers guarded the entrance. They all did a double take when Jake appeared.

'We have a breach!' exclaimed one guard over his helmet's internal headset.

The lights in the hospital went out before he got the first word out. In the darkness Jake grinned. He had also taken the liberty of placing a virus in the computer system. He wasn't skilled at creating such things using his powers, but it was something primitive enough to cut the power to the complex when he willed it.

The Enforcers saw Dark Hunter consumed by darkness. Then two baneful red eyes appeared. They swung their guns in his direction.

Green radioactive whips lashed out. One Enforcer was struck down. Another two had the barrels of their automatic rifles sliced in half before they could fire a shot. The other two Enforcers opened fire.

The Last Battle

They saw the red eyes bob towards them. Seconds later, lit by the waxing moonlight, Jake appeared at their side. Jake's hands glowed green and his heat-touch melted both the rifles in the Enforcers' hands. Then both men were hurled across the quad.

A pair of powerful searchlights mounted on the corners of the quad clunked to life, powered by the back-up generator. More Enforcers were positioned on the roof.

Jake grabbed the nearest man to him and super-hurled him through the air. The poor guard smashed into the searchlight, blotting it out. Jake had anticipated the back-up. He psychically connected to the virus he had placed into the computer system and disabled the back-up generator, killing the second light.

Gunfire opened up along the lip of the quad. The three conscious Enforcers screamed at their companions to cease fire. Jake had already pushed his way through the entrance, dragging the sliding doors open and forcing them closed so hard that the glass cracked. That didn't bother Jake. His temper was boiling, kept just on the verge of freaking out; it allowed him access to the cauldron of powers within his system. He tapped the glass and it turned instantly to stone, creating a barrier against the Enforcers outside.

He silently thanked Basilisk, whose power had only worked on organic matter. Jake's body had tweaked it enough to work on anything, all without his conscious intervention.

He ran down the dark corridor; his red vision showed him the path ahead. He remembered every twist and turn from memory. It was eerily silent, but he knew the lack of alarms was due to the power cut. Eric Kirby and his men would be panicking.

Fifteen Enforcers ran from a side corridor and spotted him instantly through their nightvision goggles. The gunfire came straight away.

High-calibre bullets impacted into an opaque shield that Jake had formed with one hand. The mass of the bullets forced him to take several steps back. The shield blocked him from firing back at the guards. It was stalemate.

The effort required to keep the shield up was taking its toll. His legs were shaking. He needed to think strategically about the situation. Wearing himself out now would only prevent him from getting through the next obstacle.

On impulse, he formed a new power. He had no idea how his body re-engineered the necessary superpowers based on his will, but it did. He felt his eyes opening so wide it was painful. Then a blinding strobe light flickered from them.

The Last Battle

For the fifteen men wearing nightvision goggles it was like staring into the sun. They all shrieked and covered their eyes. Three continued to fire but only succeeded in injuring their own men.

Jake dispelled his shield and marched down the corridor. That was the strategy element—now it was time for brute force.

He punched, kicked, and elbowed his way through the blinded Enforcers. Not once did he relent with his super-strength.

Bodies were hurled through plasterboard walls, smashed into the floor tiles; and one was thrown so hard through the ceiling that he was wedged there, hanging from his shoulders, his feet kicking out.

Jake made it to the stairwell. Another figure ran down the steps towards him. It was a doctor. Jake was too wound up to notice. He blasted the doctor backwards with a radioactive streamer—only realizing his mistake afterwards.

The man groaned, his white jacket charred and smouldering. At least he was still alive. Jake ignored a flicker of guilt. He had to get up to the second floor but could hear the clattering of boots from more Enforcers running down to greet him.

Jake looked around for another means of escape. He eyed the ceiling and hoped his next plan would work. He flew upwards—phasing through the ceiling.

He shot from the floor—right through a squad of Enforcers who were joining more filing down the staircase. The golden rule of phasing through objects was to know what was on the other side of the obstruction so you didn't solidify in the middle of a table or worse still, another person.

Jake couldn't avoid passing through the middle of an Enforcer. He strained, keeping focused on not solidifying—that would fuse them together, killing them both. The man screamed from the unpleasant experience. Jake had it worse—his eyes were open and he could see every detail of the man's internal organs and bone structure as he moved through him. It was the most unpleasant thing he had ever done.

Then he was out and phasing into the corridor above. Jake became solid again, landing on the floor. He heard yelling from the stairwell next to him. The Enforcers were now below Jake, but had realized what he'd done.

Jake summoned an enormous black fireball in his hands. He hurled it at the staircase. Concrete and metal buckled in the inferno—and the entire staircase collapsed down on the Enforcers.

Jake ran down the dark corridor—his goal lay around the corner. He rounded it and studied the new threat.

The boy and girl guarding the door looked about

eighteen; they were Downloaders. They stood to rigid attention, no doubt taking Kirby's orders dead seriously. They stared at Jake with round eyes.

'Dark Hunter!' exclaimed the girl.

Jake got little satisfaction from his infamy; he was trying to work out what powers these two clowns had downloaded.

The boy charged towards him, jumping through the air. Mid-leap his entire body shapeshifted into a huge jaguar. Jake was too surprised to react. The jaguar landed on Jake's chest and he felt the talons dig deep, drawing blood. Jake moaned in pain. He felt another slash at his stomach, this one deep and painful.

Jake booted the big cat off. The animal bumped into the ceiling so hard the shock transformed it back into the boy—who fell down, hard. The boy tried to scramble to his feet—but Jake flexed his hand and encased the boy in the same amber crystal he had used to trap Chameleon.

'Stan!' yelled the girl in a distraught voice.

Jake got to his feet and wobbled. He was sickened to see that the slash marks had ripped his stomach open— and his intestines spilled out. He dropped to his knees, scrambling to shove them back into his body.

He wailed from the pain and the knowledge that he was handling his own internal organs. He willed his healing factor to kick in, but the wound was deep and he was frightfully weak.

The girl crouched for an attack—and Jake was surprised to see a snake-like tail arc over her head and smash into the floor next to him.

Jake glanced down at his wound—it was now healing unusually fast. The folds of flesh sealed together so quickly he had to yank his fingers away to prevent the wound healing around them. He looked back up to see—

The prehensile tail slugged him across the side of the face. Jake hit the wall, dazed. The tail wrapped around his waist and hoisted him into the air. He felt the breath sucked out of him as the tail constricted, breaking his ribs.

'This is for Stan!' yelled the girl.

Flames appeared in her hands. The intention was clear—she was going to fry Jake.

Jake had had enough. He wouldn't live through another attack. He relaxed his body—which turned into fine sand-like particles that slipped through her constricting tail and reformed as Jake when they hit the floor.

The girl had already extended her hands—jets of fire blazed from her palms like a dragon's breath. She hadn't noticed Jake had slipped from her grasp.

With no strength to fight, Jake repeated the crystal

trick—encasing the girl before she knew what had hit her. He stopped himself from smashing her apart—reaching his parents was more important.

Jake slammed the ward door open and immediately spotted his mum and dad lying on beds. They were pale and unconscious. A battery of machines monitored their health—but the waves looked feeble.

He ran towards them . . . then faltered. He hadn't noticed the three figures standing at the far end of the room.

'Congratulations,' said Eric Kirby stepping forward. 'I see you've finally perfected manufacturing powers at will. I bet you can do almost anything.'

Jake was speechless. His parents were metres away but he didn't possess the strength to reach them. He had failed.

Munir and Beth flanked Kirby.

'I think you deserve some kind of award,' said Munir. 'You've crippled the Council of Evil, helped expose Grimm for the wretch he was and then returned willingly back to us.'

'I still want my revenge,' snapped Beth and stepped forward.

Kirby held up his hand to stop her.

'All in good time.' His eyes never left Jake. 'I'm aware your powers can no longer be neutralized, but I think even you wouldn't dare open fire around

them.' He jerked a bony finger towards Jake's parents. 'And I wouldn't even think of trying to escape.'

There was the sound of movement behind Jake. He gasped in shock. Chameleon was standing in the doorway. He didn't disguise the fact he wanted to kill Jake. Worse still, Lorna was at his side.

Jake felt sick. This was truly the end. Surrounded by five superheroes, too weak to fight them, and within reach of saving his parents.

It had all been for nothing.

He felt tears roll down his cheek.

'Jake?' Lorna approached him.

'Leave me alone,' he snarled. She had shown her true colours and there was no way he could reconcile the differences between them.

'Careful, Lorna,' warned Kirby.

'He won't harm me,' said Lorna confidently.

She reached out and took Jake's unresisting hand in hers. Then she did something entirely unexpected.

Lorna forced Jake's hand around her throat and spun round so that he was now holding her tight against him as a shield. She screamed loudly and the four other heroes tensed for combat—but they couldn't while one of their own was in the way.

'Help! He's got me!' wailed Lorna.

Jake was puzzled. What the hell was she doing? Before he could speak he felt Lorna shudder.

'He's leeching my powers!'

Jake suddenly understood. Lorna was trying to help him, giving him the chance to obtain some powers! Although she hadn't downloaded them from Villain.net, which incorporated Jake's own DNA and made him an addict, he could still get the buzz from any other power—Munir had proved that.

His hand pressed hard against Lorna's neck and he drained her powers. He felt the immediate benefit, his senses no longer felt numb and cloudy and his legs stopped shaking. He assumed the role of ruthless hostage taker.

'If anyone moves I'll kill her!'

He edged towards his parents.

Beth pushed forward. 'No! Don't let him touch them!'

Kirby and Munir held her back. Jake locked eyes with Kirby, mentally daring him to tell her the truth. Kirby knew he wasn't going to harm his parents, although he probably thought he would kill Lorna.

'Nobody move!' commanded Kirby. 'Don't hurt Lorna. She has done nothing to you.'

'She was a spy!' Jake had now positioned himself between both beds.

'She had no idea what she was getting herself into. She was shocked, heartbroken even, to discover that you are a villain. I was the one who sent her back to your side, against her will. It was the only way to get close to you.'

Jake saw the sentiment in Kirby's eyes and knew Kirby was speaking the truth. That meant Lorna had genuinely stumbled across his secret. It also meant that the old fool cared about Lorna. Jake's confidence increased, his old bully instincts knew exactly what buttons to press.

'I don't believe you. You know I wouldn't think twice about ripping her throat out!'

Lorna gave a strangled scream for effect. Jake touched his mother's brow. She felt cold and clammy. Beth tried to move, but Kirby and Munir held her back.

'What are you doing?' she demanded.

'Trying to help them!'

Jake felt the cure he had taken from Pete sink into his mum. It was quickly followed by the remnants of Psych's power that contained her stolen memories— the one vital component Jake was unable to create. He repeated the process with his dad. Beth was sobbing . . . then she suddenly stopped.

The life support machines started registering stronger vitals. Jake couldn't stop the smile breaking across his face. Then both parents woke up as if from a deep slumber. They glanced around the ward in confusion.

'Where am I?' said his mum in a surprisingly firm

voice. She saw Beth first, wearing her black jumpsuit.
'Bethany? What on earth are you wearing?'

Beth yelped with delight.

'Hello, son.' Jake turned to see his dad had propped
himself up on his elbows.

'Dad?' Jake's voice was strained. 'You remember
me?'

'Of course I remember you, Jake. What happened?
Why are we in hospital?'

'What are you doing to that girl, Jake?' asked his
mum cautiously. She now had full memories of the
mischief Jake got himself into.

Jake wanted to throw his arms around them both—
but knew the moment he released Lorna the four
superheroes would tear him apart. Beth stared at Jake
in confusion.

'What have you done to my parents? Mum, Dad?
This isn't your son. You don't have one!'

'Of course we do,' chided Mum. 'He's your older
brother. What's got into you?'

Jake was bursting to tell them what had happened,
but it was slowly dawning on him that he was still
trapped. Now his strength was renewed he could tunnel straight out, but he had no idea how he would
explain that to his parents. Beth was another problem;
he had to touch her to find a way to restore her
memory. He hoped that Kirby would be forced to do it,

now their parents' memories had been fully regained. Jake felt some satisfaction that Kirby had no way of wiping their minds again, as Psych had been killed and he had extracted the last of the power from Pete.

'Chameleon, stand next to the others,' said Jake in a firm voice.

Chameleon slowly joined Kirby. Jake backed to the door, keeping Lorna close.

'What are you doing?' demanded his dad. 'Are you in some sort of trouble?'

'I'll explain later, Dad. Right now I have to go.'

He dearly wanted to stay, wanted to say more, but he couldn't. He edged into the corridor.

'Let Lorna go,' said Kirby.

'I go first,' replied Jake. He edged into the corridor, giving his parents one last look. Then he backed into the corridor, out of their line of sight. He whispered into Lorna's ear.

'Thank you. Make sure my family's treated well.'

She felt his hand disappear from her throat and a faint swish as he quantum tunnelled away. The four heroes raced into the corridor and Lorna had the good sense to collapse onto the floor.

Kirby shouted with frustration. Jake had escaped.

A week had passed and Jake had regained strength by

downloading from Villain.net. He relaxed back in his own private chamber in the Council of Evil.

With his castle destroyed he had nowhere to return to, and while the Hero Foundation still stood, he couldn't return home.

He was surprised to be treated as a hero, or anti-hero at least, by Necros and the remaining Council members. Word had reached them that Jake had uncovered the assassins to be Grimm and Momentum—the founders of Forge. Forge itself had been scattered, although from the few reports that Jake had received, it appeared that Pete was attempting to lead them as his own private army.

Jake pondered Pete's future as that was still in his hands and he wanted to see Pete suffer for what he had done. But he might have a use for Pete in the future, even if his powers had a shelf life. Did that mean Jake's did too? He tried not to think about it. For now, Pete was safe.

Jake had spun the facts to make him sound like the Council's saviour. He told Necros that straight after Grimm and Momentum had taken out the Council's relay station he had destroyed their super-weapon. He hadn't told them that he was integral to the weapon as that would lead to too many awkward questions.

Abyssal was cleared of any charges of trying to overthrow the Council and blame was placed at

Momentum's door. The frozen remains of the supervillain had been found near the wreckage of Jake's castle. Munir had been merciless in finishing the villain off.

The island's ambassadors conducted an investigation into Grimm's business and they unearthed numerous suspicious accounts of his double-dealings.

Jake enjoyed the attention, and welcomed using Momentum and Grimm as scapegoats. However, his thoughts drifted back to his parents. Now they had their memories back he longed to see them again. He hoped that Kirby had had the courtesy to restore Beth's memory and use strong raw healing powers to re-grow her hand, now that they had no use for her.

He hadn't heard from Lorna either. That was no surprise, but he did keep checking his mobile phone just in case. She was probably worried that all her communications were being monitored and couldn't risk associating herself with Jake. He missed her a lot. More than he thought he would. She had risked everything to help him and asked for nothing in return.

She had also helped the world's most wanted villain escape. What kind of hero did that make her?

Jake laughed to himself: she was *his* hero.

He was starting to get restless and hankering for some mischief now he had finally mastered the powers Basilisk had given him many months ago.

He had no ticking clock, no impending sense of

The Last Battle

dread that he was losing his family. Jake could afford to use his villainous powers for his own ends, as he had planned all that time ago when he had clicked on a spam email inviting him to rule the world.

Jake pondered what dastardly plan he should unfold. He still intended to destroy the Council of Evil and the destruction of the Hero Foundation had suddenly leapt to the top of his priorities. The question was: how?

He laid out the three pendants, which he'd taken from the fallen Council leaders, on his desk. He recalled Leech's words that six of them held the secrets of a Core Power. Jake thought back to the last moments in the hospital when Kirby had thought he would kill Lorna. Jake had caught sight of a similar pendant around Kirby's neck.

Jake drum-rolled his fingers on the table. A plan was forming.

For once, things were really starting to work for him.

Andy Briggs was born in Liverpool, England. Having endured many careers, ranging from pizza delivery and running his own multimedia company to teaching IT and film-making (though not all at the same time), he eventually remembered the constant encouragement he had received at an early age about his writing. That led him to launch himself on a poor, unsuspecting Hollywood. In between having fun writing movie scripts, Andy now has far too much fun writing novels.

He lives in a secret lair somewhere in the south-east of England—attempting to work despite his three crazy cats. His claims about possessing superpowers may be somewhat exaggerated . . .

Power Surge is his third novel in the deviously dark 'Villain.net' series, and follows *Rise of the Heroes*, *Virus Attack*, and *Crisis Point* in the fiendishly clever 'Hero.com' anti-series.

Wondering about the
heroes' side of things?

Well check out

HERO.COM 3 –
CRISIS
POINT

Available now.
Get your hands on it!